Dealing with the Devil
By Marina Black

I0538370

ISBN: 978-0-9966486-1-5

This book is dedicated to my Internet wife.

When I started writing, this story was a vague blur of ideas running around in my head. With J's guidance, support, and saint-level patience, I am now publishing my very first original novel. I wouldn't be here today without you, JoJo. You are my cheerleader, my sounding board, and my editor (for the low, low price of Momopoly dollars and unflattering selfies, I might add). I would also like to take this opportunity to offer a huge apology to J's husband and kids, who might've forgotten what her attention feels like since I have clearly been hogging all of it. Y- I owe you a beer, buddy. You are a wonderful man!

To my other *Pantskru* ladies, you are the <u>bomb</u>. Without our wonderfully bizarre e-mail chains and obsession with primetime television shows, my life would have no meaning. I love ya'll so very much.

I'd also like to thank my awesome family. Mom, all those notebooks you bought me have finally paid off. Dad, thanks for deferring that loan payment again. To my brother and sister, you guys are awesome. I am the person I am today because of you guys! You can take that as a compliment or not...I'm going to leave it open ended. ☺

Finally, if you've made it to the end of this dedication page, I'd also like to thank you. You are a real trooper for making it through all that sappiness! I'm glad you're still here. Without further ado, please enjoy *Dealing With the Devil*.

Love,
Marina

Chapter One

Lucy Harding leaned her full weight against the ancient linoleum countertop at Marge's Diner. The cogs of the antique wall clock clicked with every second that passed, wearing away the little patience Lucy had left. She rubbed at the dark purple stain of exhaustion beneath her eyes and exhaled sharply. Her fingers dragged through her ebony hair in a vain attempt to smooth a bit of the frizz. What was the use? It was a steamy, sticky July morning in the middle of the Nevada desert. Not to mention, it was ass crack o'clock and most of the world was still in bed. There wasn't anyone around to judge Lucy for looking like a ragamuffin.

This is the lot you chose in life, Lucy reminded herself. She inhaled the crisp, buttery scent of her brand new leather vest. It was this cut that distinguished her as a prospect with the Devil's Own Motorcycle Club. Joining the local MC was pretty much the only thing to do in the tiny, shit sack town called Errol. In the entire history of the MC, they had never accepted a female. Hell, they'd never even *prospected* one. Lucy Harding wasn't just any female, though. She was family, legacy, and above all, she was a big fucking joke.

Last night, James "Monster" Walcott used his proxy votes to push through a majority that afforded Lucy her shot at being a real member of the Devil's Own. Everyone knew Monster's aim was to get back at Lucy's brother for all the hell he raised. Danny

Harding was forever acting like a jackass; it was a miracle that he had even been allowed to remain a member after all the antics he pulled. The MC turned a blind eye to Danny's behavior because their father had once been President of the club. Hell, the Hardings could trace their lineage back three generations—longer than any other Devil in the club. If Danny could get away with murder just because of his last name, Lucy wasn't going to let chauvinistic misogynists tell her that she couldn't just because she had to sit down to pee. She was a Harding and that *meant* something.

"Here ya' go, darlin'…" The waitress's raspy voice dragged Lucy out of her thoughts. Lucy dug into her purse for a couple loose bills and tossed them down on the counter. "Keep the change, thanks." Carefully, she stacked the trays of coffee on top of one another and held her breath all the way to the car. It took some maneuvering to set the coffee onto the floorboards of the aged Cadillac without spilling it all over. This old girl had been in the family for longer than she could remember. Lucy had learned to drive behind this steering wheel; she'd sat in the passenger seat and watched the world go by while her mother ran errands. Hell, this was the same car they brought her home from the hospital in just after she was born. Clunker or not, the sentimental value was worth the risk Lucy took every time she drove it. Besides, it wasn't as if she could carry twelve coffees back to the clubhouse on her Harley.

The air outside was sticky and thick but the AC in the car had shit out long ago. Lucy ached to feel the wind on her face as she zoomed down the open road on her bike. Instead, she coughed at the exhaust fumes and ignored the shrieking brakes as she backed out onto the dusty road.

The Devil's clubhouse doubled as a bar and despite the obscenely early hour, more than a dozen bikes were parked outside in a messy line. After the new prospects had been voted on last night, there had been a massive party. Sleeping bodies were strewn over every corner of the place in various states of undress. Lucy rolled her eyes at the sight of her brother snuggled between two Devil Eaters. It was a damn miracle he hadn't ended up with half a dozen kids by now. Lucy shook her head in disgust. Whatever Danny saw in those sluts, Lucy would never understand it. She kept hoping one day he'd wake up and realize the mistakes he'd made. Until then, he'd better be careful. Lucy was not ready to be an aunt...

The sun rose higher and soft yellow light streamed through the blinds. Pretty soon the club members would wake—cranky and hung over—but there would be coffee, at least. Lucy had done her duty. When she caught sight of her reflection in the plate glass window, she swore bitterly. Battling against naturally curly hair that hadn't been washed in two days was one fight Lucy knew she was going to lose. She needed a shower and a nap—not necessarily in that order. Since things were settled for the moment,

Lucy stifled a yawn and turned to head out when she slammed face first into a very broad, muscular chest. The scent of leather, sandalwood, and musk filled her nose and Lucy knew instinctively who she'd run into.

Gabriel Archer—"Archie," as he preferred to be called—stood half a foot taller than Lucy and easily dwarfed her not-so-diminutive five foot nine inch frame. The man was built like a pro wrestler: rippling muscles covered every inch of him. He had large, rough hands, and his cobalt eyes glinted coldly as he glared down at Lucy. His expression was alight with fire and the muscle in his jaw ticked as he gritted his teeth. Archie was the kind of guy whose physical presence terrified others and instantly commanded respect. Lucy, however, had grown up at his side and knew he was a gentle giant; she also refused to call him by his silly nickname, which always irked him.

Gabe was the first boy who pulled her pigtails on the playground; he also took on the role of the husband when they played house. Although they were once thick as thieves, Lucy couldn't deny their dynamic had changed over the years as they grew up and apart. Still, she knew if anyone messed with her, Gabe would be right there to defend her. Until now...

Lucy's onyx eyes traveled upward until they met his. *Oh shit*, she thought to herself. Gabe had been away for the majority of the week, visiting with other Presidents from the Devil's sister charters.

Given his state of dishevelment, he'd ridden all night to get home.

"What the hell are you wearing?" Archie thundered, "If someone sees you in that cut they're going to think you're a prospect..."

Lucy crossed her arms over her chest. She widened her stance, as if preparing for a fight. "I *am* a prospect, Gabriel. I won the vote last night fair and square."

"No way in hell!" Archie roared. The boom of his voice caused several of the sleeping MC members to jump up from their positions. Beaver's hand was already sitting on his gun, ready to fire if necessary. When the rest of them realized this was more of a domestic dispute, the clubhouse started clearing out immediately.

Archie peered down at Lucy and his heart twisted in his chest. The MC was no place for a woman—especially not one like her. He had watched Lucy grow from a tiny, buck-toothed menace into a gorgeous woman. She was fierce and loyal but there was a tenderness about her; she always put the people she loved first. If he was being perfectly honest with himself—and that was rarely the case—he cared about Lucy as more than a surrogate sister. Archie ached to be with her...but there were far too many obstacles in his path. The most obvious hindrance was a six foot five inch hothead named Daniel Harding.

Danny was rabidly protective of his sister and had gotten into countless fistfights over it. Archie decided it was better to ice Lucy out, push her away, and stop her from invading his life. The less they saw each other, the less he had to deny how much he wanted her and how deeply he already cared. "This has to be some kind of joke. Nobody in their right fucking mind would patch you unless they have a goddamn death wish!"

Lucy's anger rose steadily, spilling outward as she squared off with him. She had no doubt that once Gabe got his hands on Monster, there would be hell to pay. Hopefully, she could soften the blow a bit beforehand. "What's the big deal? You and Danny both prospected and got patched. Why can't I?" Planting her hands firmly on her hips, she stared him down. "And if you say it's because I'm a woman, so help me God, I will kick your ass all the way back to the dark ages!"

"Lucy!" Archie cried in exasperation. His demeanor darkened as he closed the distance between them. Grasping her shoulders, he stared deep into her fathomless eyes. "This is *not* the life for you. You deserve better than this!"

Ignoring the searing heat from his palms that seeped through her jacket, Lucy swallowed back the attraction that rose up in her every time he was near. "Don't I deserve to be a part of something that's been so vital to my family for so long? The MC

8

is my life. Danny, my parents, *you*," She retorted. "You know me, Gabriel! Two and a half kids in the suburbs isn't the life for me. I *need* this."

"You're going to get yourself killed, damn it!" Archie cried. Lucy was going to get *him* killed. How the hell could he ever focus when all he could do was wonder if she was going to be the next casualty in the turf war they were fighting against the Black Jacks? "Lucy—"

"Save it! I got the same damn speech from Danny last night. You're not my brother! You can't tell me what to do!" Lucy snapped. "Go ahead and be a hypocrite. Strip me of my patch before you even give me a shot but I'll fight you, Gabriel. I've been over those bylaws a thousand times and it doesn't say a woman can't patch!" She snapped, "You will have to take this all the way to the damn original charter if you want to keep me down!" Lucy's anger reached fevered pitch as she stomped toward the door. Between her exhaustion and Archie's condescension, she couldn't stand it another minute.

Archie slammed his fist down against the table as Lucy left the clubhouse. Dragging in a ragged breath, he counted to ten...then kept on going. Anger curled in his gut and spread like wildfire through his veins. Turning, he stalked into the bar where some of the boys were still sleeping it off. "I want Monster in the War Room, *now*! If he's not in there within the next ten minutes, you will all suffer the consequences!"

Everyone left sleeping was shattered from their slumbers and scattered to the wind.

Slamming the door closed with far more force than was necessary, Archie grabbed one of the coffees that Lucy bought and took a sip. Pinching the bridge of his nose, he stared down at the Devil's Own skull and crossbones insignia carved into the War Room table. Lucy was his personal temptress and his tormentor. This whole scenario only played out one of two ways and Lucy would end up hurt no matter what. Archie swore then and there, he'd do anything to keep her safe. He would be damned if she suffered one ounce of pain. How the fuck was he going to survive this?

Chapter Two

The slamming of the front door startled Lucy out of a fitful sleep. After leaving the clubhouse, she went straight home but she was far too keyed up to rest. It took an extremely hot shower and a cup of chamomile to put a dent in the rage that roiled inside her. Gabriel Archer was *infuriating*. He got under her skin and burrowed in deep, keeping her flushed and off-center. If not for the crushing exhaustion of being up for twenty-seven hours straight, Lucy would never have been able to fall asleep. Once she had, her mind immediately slipped back to simpler times...

Lucy remembered the exact moment her relationship with Gabriel changed forever. Every year, Lucy and her mother would spend several weeks visiting family in California while the boys ran hog wild. Right before Lucy's sixteenth birthday, her mother insisted she spend her entire school vacation with her cousins in Oakland. That fateful summer, Lucy left Errol as an awkward, clumsy adolescent and came home a woman. Almost overnight she had grown into her height and her voluptuous curves. Danny didn't tease her quite as much either. Instead, he grew fiercely defensive of his little sister and sent every potential suitor running for the hills. Gabe stopped walking her home after school and snuggling next to her on the couch when they watched TV. Instead, he began to treat her with a cold indifference that had spanned the last ten years...

"Lucy!" Danny busted into her room without knocking. His fists were tight with rage. "Archie's on the fucking warpath! What the *hell* did you do to him?" Daniel Harding was almost exactly the opposite of Lucy in every way. While she had inherited their mother's dark hair and eyes, Danny was blonde and blue-eyed like their Irish/English father. Despite how monumentally different they looked, the one feature they shared was the legendary Harding temper.

Swinging her legs over the side of the bed, Lucy abruptly stood. Danny was much taller than her but he was well aware Lucy could hold her own in a fight, especially since she wasn't afraid to fight dirty. "I told Gabriel *exactly* what he needed to hear. I'm

11

not backing down from this and there's nothing either of you can do to stop me!" She brushed past Danny on her way into the kitchen.

As usual, Danny was hot on her heels. Lucy ignored him as she dug through the cabinets for anything that wasn't Ramen noodles and came up empty handed. After their parents died, Danny had stepped in as Lucy's guardian for six months before she turned eighteen but the legal arrangement couldn't have been further from the truth. It was *always* Lucy who took care of Danny. She assumed full responsibility of the shopping, cooking, cleaning, and washing that had to get done in the house. Lucy made sure Danny got up for work and the bills were paid on time. She even went so far as to make sure there were always condoms in the house—which was well outside the realm of duties a caring sister should have to deal with. Now, her new status as a prospect meant things were going to change. Lucy wouldn't be Danny's keeper anymore. The sooner he realized that, the better.

"This is seriously fucked up, Luce…" Danny deflated, slumping down in a chair at the kitchen table. "It's too dangerous." He'd seen way too many women chewed up and spit out by the MC that weren't even prospects. It would be so much worse for Lucy. He couldn't bear the thought of his little sister getting hurt. "What would mom say if she could see you now? You're better than the rest of us, Lucy! You always were…you could actually get out of this town, if you wanted to. God knows you're fucking persistent as hell."

"Mom can't see me now because the Black Jacks gunned her and daddy down in the street," Lucy replied coldly. "The club is my legacy, Danny. I'm not leaving Errol or my family behind." After putting a pot of coffee on, she settled beside her brother. "I know you want to protect me but I'm not a little girl anymore. I can take care of myself." Meeting Danny's worried gaze, she gently rested her hand on his wrist. "I prospect for a year before you all vote on my patch. Give me a chance," Lucy pleaded. "That's all I ask, Danny. *One* chance."

Danny closed his eyes for half a second and slumped in defeat. "There isn't anything I can do to stop you. Unless you really fuck up, my hands are tied. But don't think for a second I'm going to take it easy on you just because you're my sister."

"I wouldn't have it any other way." The coffee was nearly ready, filling the quaint kitchen with the heavenly aroma of hazelnut. "I'm going to run by the store before the meeting tonight. If you want something, make sure it's on the list." She was back in sister mode now. "And *please* take a shower?"

Shaking his head in annoyance, Danny poured himself a cup of coffee as he trotted toward his room. In his eyes, Lucy would always be the buck toothed little girl who followed him everywhere and drove him insane. Seeing her wearing that cut burned so deeply inside him… he'd have to let things run their course but that didn't mean he had to fight fair. Danny had already made up his mind: there was no way Lucy was ever going to be a Devil and that was final.

Chapter Three

Lucy ignored the not-so-hushed whispers that erupted the minute she walked into the War Room that afternoon. Danny was already sitting down at the complete opposite side of the table as Monster, who was sporting a painful looking black eye. To Danny's left was Beaver—a heavily bearded transfer from their charter in Ontario. Wilson, Big Mike, and PJ had already taken their places and were taking turns glaring at Lucy as she inched toward the last seat available: the one right next to Gabe.

Archie tightened his fist around the gavel in his hand and squelched the urge to jam it down Monster's throat. The man had already paid in full for his actions, according to their charter's laws but Archie was hardly satisfied. Were he were a less disciplined man, Monster would be dead right now instead of just sore.

"Alright, settle down," Archie snarled, banging the wooden gavel with far more force than was necessary. "First order of business is welcoming our new prospects to their very first meeting." He cast a sidelong glance at the woman seated at his right hand, "Congratulations to Kyle, Hunter, Mort…"

Archie let out a labored breath; it pained him to even say her name. "And Lucy." The hoots and applause from the other members only made him angrier. "Patching with the Devil's Own MC is an honor and you should treat that cut with the same respect you show your mother. When you're wearing our colors, you represent every man in this room—"

"Every woman too," Lucy added. She watched Gabe's blood pressure rise as the stain of his anger darkened his face. Danny was glaring daggers at her. Lucy half expected Gabe to grab her by the collar and scream until he was hoarse...but he turned and continued on as if he hadn't heard her at all.

"Second order of business, now that our prospects have been welcomed properly, it's important to understand that you are the bitches of this group. If a member tells you to do something, you do it and you do not ask questions! If I ask you to cut off your own balls and serve them to me on a platter, you better damn well do it. Do I make myself clear?" Archie's booming voice seemed to echo throughout the room. He glared at each one of the prospects. The three boys had enough sense to look properly terrified but Lucy, of course, barely batted an eye. Her nonchalance infuriated him. "Get the fuck out of this room! You're not members yet and you don't get to be part of any club business unless I say so! You four start cleaning the bar and I'd better be able to eat off it by the time this meeting is over!"

15

Mort, Hunter, and Kyle scrambled out of the room like scared jackrabbits. Lucy, on the other hand, sauntered toward the door. She said nothing, ignoring Gabe's angry glare as she pulled the door closed behind her. Gabriel Archer could huff and puff all he wanted but he was never going to break her.

The bar was in shambles thanks to last night's festivities. Empty glasses and broken bottles covered the counters and floors, trash overflowed the garbage cans, and every surface in the place was sticky for reasons Lucy didn't care to think about. The boys stood there looking dumfounded and unsure, so she took it upon herself to hand out assignments. To their credit, not one of them argued and quickly set about completing their tasks. Mort picked up cans and bottles to be recycled, Hunter grabbed a broom and started sweeping, and Kyle helped Lucy rearrange the bar and wipe down the tables.

"That was pretty ballsy, what you did in there." Kyle chuckled as he used a cloth to brush broken glass into a trashcan. He was an inch taller than Lucy and his dark hair had been chopped into a crew cut. Warm brown eyes sparkled with mirth, radiating warmth and goodness. He collected more glasses and brought them over to be washed.

Lucy looked up from the pile of snifters she was cleaning and smirked. "Gabe doesn't scare me," She replied. "He's a good President. He's strong and

16

cunning and he believes in the club...but he also takes archaic traditions far too seriously. The MC has been a boys club for way too long."

Kyle grabbed a towel and started to dry the glasses Lucy had already cleaned. He nodded cordially, "I just think you're brave, is all. If anyone's going to break the glass ceiling, it's definitely going to be you." He flashed her a handsome smile. Once he finished drying, Kyle trotted over to help Mort carry a huge bag of recyclables out to the bin. By the time he got back, Lucy was putting the last of the glasses back onto the shelf. The bar was cleaner than it had been even *before* the party, though no one in their right mind would ever eat off the floor.

The meeting didn't last too much longer. Pretty soon, members poured out of the War Room, rowdy and thirsty. Mort got behind the bar and immediately started serving up drinks. Kyle and Hunter were ordered to suit up and head to the border to make sure no Black Jacks crossed into the territory during the night. Lucy was left to wash down the rest of the tables. She was leaning over to scrub a spot at the bar when she felt a shadow creep behind her. Seconds later, Lucy cried out as she was rammed against the bar. "What the hell!"

"I usually like my women with more meat on them but for now, you're gonna to have to do." Beaver's breath smelled heavily of tequila; it was obvious he had been drinking long before the meeting took place. He chuckled derisively and pushed her again, this time toward the rooms in the back, "You heard what Archie said. You have to do whatever I say without question. And I say you're gonna suck my dick, sweetheart." Beaver turned slightly to the left and swallowed a mouthful of fist.

The veins in Gabriel's neck throbbed so noticeably that Lucy was terrified they were going to burst. The massive man reached down to finish beating the life out of Beaver when Lucy grabbed Gabe's arm. "Stop!" Lucy was still startled from being grabbed but she forced herself to regain her bearings. "You told him not even an hour ago that I'm a prospect and I have to do whatever he asks without question."

"What he's asking you to do isn't right, Lucy!" Archie thundered. This was everything he had feared...Lucy was beautiful, delicate, and sweet and these men were going to ruin her. "Do you want to suck his fucking dick?"

"Of course I don't!" Lucy cried, "But I expect to be treated just like any other prospect. Which means I shouldn't need to worry about being asked to perform sexual favors! If I couldn't finish the job, would Mort be asked to step in? How about Hunter or Kyle?" Lucy gritted her teeth angrily. "I don't think so!" Despite her best efforts, her entire body shook in rage and fear. She was aware of the possibility that someone might try and take advantage of her position; she simply hadn't expected it to happen so soon.

Beaver crawled away while Lucy and Archie stared each other down. There was no doubt that Archie had busted the man's nose. Meanwhile, he was left with such overwhelming guilt. Archie *had* told everyone the prospects had to do whatever they were told, without question; it was just the way things worked in the MC. They'd all been hazed during their induction and each one of them survived. Then again, he'd kill anyone who so much as looked at Lucy sideways. This was just another reason why she didn't belong here. "I guess I need to make it clear that demanding sex from a prospect is not acceptable..." He growled at those who were assembled, "Although I really wish I didn't have to!" He exhaled sharply as he struggled to rein in his emotions. "Go home, Luce. I'll deal with you later."

Lucy's eyes narrowed into angry slits. What the hell did he mean *deal with her later*? Gabe had the look of a man on the edge. She thought about arguing but given precarious nature of the situation, she grabbed her purse from behind the bar and did what she was told. On her way out, Danny grabbed her arm; she could feel concern radiating off him in waves. Lucy flashed Danny half a smile. "I'm fine. Don't worry about me." Danny didn't look convinced but Lucy *was* fine. Their father hadn't allowed her to be a weakling. If Beaver tried to force her into anything, she'd have made a eunuch out of him in ten seconds flat.

Hitting the open road was just what Lucy needed right now. Her Harley seemed petite next to the hulking bikes parked outside the club. The streetlights reflected against the shimmering cherry red paint, polished to perfection. Lucy loved this bike more than she could ever imagine loving anything else in the world. The wheel wells were perfectly pristine and spotless, the handlebars free of any dust or debris, and the engine purred like a kitten as she turned the key. Once her helmet was fastened securely, Lucy took off like a shot.

She considered taking the long way home when thunder rumbled in the distance. Lucy pushed harder, weaving her way along the back roads to shave off time. She made it home just as a storm kicked up around her. Rain like this meant Danny would sleep at the club tonight; it wasn't safe to be riding in this kind of weather. Plus, the Devil Eaters would be out around midnight and he never turned down an opportunity to sleep with a pretty woman.

Lightning zipped in the distance as Lucy changed out of her jeans and slipped into a pair of black yoga pants and a tank top. She desperately needed to work out some of her frustrations. The home gym wasn't much to speak of: there was a punching bag suspended on a thick metal chain, a set of free weights, and a rusty rowing machine that her mother had picked up at a garage sale before Danny was born. Lucy quickly taped her hands before taking the first hit on the punching bag. It barely swung as she warmed up but her blows became more aggressive as she hit her stride.

Perspiration beaded on Lucy's brow as she poured her frustrations into her workout. She landed a particularly hard blow and sweat burned into her eyes. Lucy cursed and grabbed a towel, dragging it over her face. When she pulled it away, she startled at the realization that she was not alone.

"Pretending this is my face?" Archie drawled lazily, grabbing the bag so it wouldn't knock her as it swung. His lips curved up into half a smile despite how unsettled things were between them right now.

Lucy padded over to the ancient fridge that stood in the corner. "Something like that…" She tugged the door open and dug around. "You want a beer?" She tossed him a can before cracking open her water and taking a long sip. "What are you doing here?"

"I need to talk to you." A rumble of thunder shook the house and the lights flickered menacingly. "But not down here. If the power goes out, I do not want to be trapped in this stuffy basement." This time when he reached for her, his touch was gentle. "I'm not here to argue, okay? Hear me out, Luce." Archie shepherded her up the stairs while trying not to stare at her delightfully rounded backside in those damned stretchy pants.

Lucy didn't protest. The power frequently went out during storms. As kids, they'd spent many nights huddled in a blanket fort in the living room with a single flashlight between them. Lucy brushed away the memories and immediately headed into the kitchen to dig that old flashlight out of a drawer. Without being asked, Gabriel lit several candles. They moved around each other with relative ease, performing monotonous tasks until finally everything was complete and they were forced to interact with one another again.

Lucy stood awkwardly before him. She examined a loose thread on her shirt, tugging at it idly to distract herself. "So..."

Archie sat down at the kitchen table and neatly folded his hands. "Have you eaten?"

A smile ghosted across Lucy's lips. "You didn't come all the way over here to ask me if I ate dinner, did you? Just say what you need to say...you're stripping me of my patch, aren't you?"

Archie exhaled sharply. "Although I would very much *like* to, rules are rules and you haven't broken any of the major ones yet." He truly wished that she had. If he were a petty man, he'd find a way to get it done...but Lucy would never forgive him and he couldn't live with that. "We've been at war with the Black Jacks for a long time. They've got all the territory around Errol locked in and we're the only thing standing in their way from controlling the state. Things have been quiet for a while but it's only a matter of time before the violence escalates again."

Both of Lucy's parents had been casualties in the war that had started long before she was ever born. She cocked her head in confusion. "Okay, tell me something I don't know?"

Archie fought to hide his smile. "Even though the Black Jacks are strong, I have it on very good authority that their hold on Reno is slipping. It's ripe for the taking, Lucy. The club voted tonight and the Devils are going to make a play for their territory."

"Jesus Christ, Gabriel, that's suicide!" Fear clawed its way into Lucy's chest. It was one thing to operate in Errol where everybody and their brother was affiliated with the MC in some way…but Reno was crawling with cops, lowlifes, and dealers looking for an excuse to spill blood. "Why are you even telling me this?" This was official club business, not something that was usually shared with prospects like Lucy.

"I can't just go in there guns blazing." Archie huffed. "I'm not a complete idiot, in case you hadn't noticed." His expression bordered on murderous as he waited for her to make a comment that never came. "I need to make my presence known in the least threatening way possible."

"Oh? And how do you intend on doing that?" Lucy asked hesitantly. Gabe had a look on his face that made her uneasy…

"It's very simple, really." Archie leaned back in his chair. "We're getting married." Another crack of lightning lit the sky, followed by a fantastic boom of thunder. In an instant, the power went down and they were bathed in darkness. As dramatic as the moment was, Archie wished that he could see the expression on Lucy's face right now.

Lucy coughed and sputtered. She couldn't have been more shocked if he'd told her they were going on a one-way trip to the moon. "I-I'm sorry. I swore you just said that we were getting married. As in *you* and *I*…"

Archie leaned in closer, his hot breath fanning over her neck as he spoke. "You wanted to be a Devil, right? This is your ticket." His voice was thick and gravelly, "If we win Reno, we could end their reign of terror. The Black Jacks would be gone for good. We need to do this and I don't care what it takes, Lucy." Archie paused, dragging a hand across his stubbled chin. "You know the rules. There are only certain things that allow a Devil to cross the border into Reno, turns out a honeymoon is one of them." He glanced at her. "And as much as I dislike it, you're the only choice. The club has already voted so…like it or not, that's the way it goes, Luce. You're a prospect. What I say goes."

Lucy's breath caught in her throat. She wanted to fight him but she was too flabbergasted to make a viable argument. There had to be *some* reason she could come up with as to why they couldn't get married, but damn if she could think of one in that moment. By the time Lucy regained her bearings, Gabriel was already heading out into the storm with her only source of light in hand. She hurried after him. "Hey! That's mine!" It was a stupid thing to say. In the scheme of things, he was taking a lot more from her than a flashlight...

"I promise you'll get it back tomorrow. I'll return it when I pick you up for the wedding. Make sure you pack enough clothes, sweetheart, because we're going on an *extended* honeymoon." Another flash of lightning illuminated Lucy's form in the doorway and despite everything, Archie smiled. This was the absolute worst idea ever. Marrying Lucy Harding would make spending time with her unavoidable. Archie wanted to push her away; it was easier to deny his feelings that way. But if playing pretend for a week or two could save the MC and the town of Errol from the Black Jacks, it was a sacrifice he was willing to make.

Lucy stood in the doorway for a long time after Gabriel drove away. The wind and rain whipped around her, chilling her to the bone. Lucy was feeling uneasy. What she wanted was to be part of the Devil's Own MC and to pave the way for other women to do the same. In the course of one day, Lucy had been hollered at, groped, and was being forced into marriage. Lucy drew in a ragged breath as she stared into the storm. "What the *hell* just happened?"

Chapter Four

The murky light of dawn found Lucy standing in front of the full-length mirror, wondering what she'd gotten herself into…

The dog days of summer were definitely upon them and last night's storm offered only temporary relief from the heat. Lucy had lain awake for hours, listening to the rumbling thunder and watching the lightning illuminate the night. Sometime around midnight the storm had cleared, leaving in its wake a fathomless stretch of inky black sky dotted with millions of stars. Lucy might have enjoyed the beauty of the moment a little more if she weren't so preoccupied.

At some point, exhaustion won Lucy over and she fell into a fitful sleep. She tossed and turned; her mind spun with the uncertainty she felt about marrying Gabe and going up against the Black Jacks. The nightmares turned her stomach, the knife dug in deeper until Lucy gripped the sheets in terror. It was almost a relief when Danny stumbled home at four and started her awake. In a futile attempt to get himself some aspirin, Danny knocked everything out of the bathroom cabinet in what Lucy could only assume was an attempt to raise the dead. She made it into the hallway just in time to keep him from landing face first on the carpet.

Once Danny was safely tucked in, Lucy decided there was no use delaying the inevitable. After putting the medicine cabinet back together, she stripped off her pajamas and stepped into the shower. Lucy basked in the blissfully scalding spray until the all the hot water was gone. By the time she got out, a dull, throbbing headache was starting at the base of her skull. Lucy needed a caffeine fix pronto. Pulling her robe closed, she padded into the kitchen.

Lucy went through the motions of making coffee on autopilot. It wasn't until she poured herself a cup of the heady brew that life began to infuse into her once more. She wrapped her hands around the mug and inhaled deeply, sighing at the comforting scent of her morning Joe. Her rapture didn't last long, though. Now that she was thinking clearly again, she had to decide what to pack on a trip to hell.

Essential items were put in the suitcase first: handgun, mace, butterfly knife, deodorant, toothbrush, underwear, and the family picture taken three months before her parent died. With those items lovingly packed, Lucy dumped the rest of her clothes into the suitcase without fanfare.

At seventeen years old, Lucy lost her mother and the only female influence in her life. Louisa Harding was dainty and glamorous; her greatest joy was dressing her daughter up like a little princess. After she died, there was no one there to needle Lucy into wearing pretty dresses or to tell her when to wear pantyhose. Anything with ruffles, lace, or frills only served to remind Lucy how out of her element she was. Since then, she stuck to the basics: jeans, t-shirts, and baggy sweatshirts. Lucy owned exactly one skirt and it remained crumpled in the back of her closet until today.

Unfortunately, the lack of dressy clothes left Lucy feeling uncomfortable. She sat on the edge of her bed contemplating whether or not she was really going to wear jeans to her own wedding. If Louisa Harding could only hear Lucy now, she'd surely roll over in her grave.

Running a hand through her damp curls, Lucy gathered her courage. She tiptoed down the hall to the room her parents once shared and paused for a moment in the doorway. She took a cleansing breath and pushed the door open. The air was musty and a thick layer of dust coated everything. Neither she nor Danny liked going into this room; it dredged up too many memories. Hell, Lucy hadn't even changed the sheets on the bed. The floral ones peeking out from beneath the down comforter were the same ones her parents had snuggled beneath the night before they died. A pang of hurt hit Lucy in the chest. She forced herself to open the closet door. The lavender scent of her mother's perfume still lingered there, although it was so faint now, Lucy was sure she imagined it.

Thumbing through the clothing that hung neatly on hangars, it felt as if Louisa would walk in at any moment, smile knowingly, and pick out a fabulous outfit for her daughter to try on. Sadly, that was not the case. Lucy located the bag she was looking hiding in the back. The sacred garment was wrapped in plastic and so pristinely preserved that Lucy almost wept. Her mother promised when Lucy got married, this dress would be hers. Lucy's great grandmother had sewn this dress by hand for her daughter's wedding day and then Louisa wore it on her wedding day. It had been passed down through generations and Lucy dreamed about the day she would get to wear it. The dress was as much Lucy's legacy as the leather cut she'd neatly folded and placed in her suitcase. This may not have been the wedding Lucy ever expected but it only seemed right to uphold the tradition...

Lucy stared at her reflection in the full-length mirror, silently assessing the stranger who stared back at her. She had been told, on several occasions, that she was pretty. Lucy wasn't sure that was true. Her hair was naturally black and, because of the wild curliness, had a tendency to frizz. Lucy swept her hair up into a delicate coif and pinned the curls to keep them from getting unruly. She'd inherited her onyx-colored eyes from her mother; they were bleary and puffy from lack of sleep. For the first time in a long time, Lucy put on a little bit of makeup— just enough to hide the dark circles staining the delicate skin beneath her eyes. With a smear of lipstick and just a hint of blush, she stepped back to assess her work. Even though Lucy knew she was not a great beauty, she would make her mother proud today.

Tugging the plastic away from the wedding dress, Lucy's heart swelled in her chest. Reverently, her fingertips traced the intricate bodice adorned by a myriad of tiny, perfect pearls. The sleeves were trimmed in silk and felt incredible against her skin. The train was fairly short but the overlay was hand-sewn lace. Easing the dress over her head, Lucy's greatest fear was that the dress wouldn't fit. She was more voluptuous than her mother...then again, when Louisa wore this dress she was already several months pregnant with Danny. Much to Lucy's relief, the fabric cradled her curves like a lover's hand.

A car door slammed and the thud of footsteps got louder as he headed into the house. Lucy knew instantly that it was Gabe; she'd have recognized his heavy tread anywhere. He made his way through the kitchen to search for her then looped toward the bedrooms. He paused when he reached the door to her parents' bedroom. Lucy watched him in the glass, memorizing his expression of awe. There were easily a hundred buttons, starting at the curve of her spine and stretching all the way up her neck. "Can you help me, please?" She asked softly.

Archie's breath caught in his throat as he drank in the sight of Lucy. Seeing her in that wedding dress almost brought him to his knees. He didn't immediately trust himself to speak but inched toward her nonetheless. Archie's fingers felt clumsy as he carefully slipped each delicate pearl button into the corresponding scalloped edge. Every once in a while he glanced up, meeting her soft gaze in the mirror. When he was finally finished, Archie stepped back and dragged a hand over his stubbled jaw. Something primal had awakened inside of him and he was having a hard time keeping it under control. "I'm...underdressed."

"You look fine." *Really fine*, Lucy thought to herself. Gabe was never sexier than when he tossed on a pair of dark blue jeans, a white button down shirt, and his leather cut. She instantly recognized the cowboy boots he had bought in high school. It had taken months of mowing lawns, delivering groceries, and odd chores to earn enough to buy them. Once he had, Gabe wore them almost every day. He kept them pristine by oiling the leather and Lucy knew for a fact he drove two hours to see a cobbler every year. If Gabe was even half as good a husband to her as he was to those boots, they would be okay.

Lucy wondered what her mother would say if she could see her preparing to marry Gabriel Archer. Lucy wanted to believe her mother would be proud— if not concerned that Gabe and Lucy were marrying for club business instead of love. "The first memory I have is of my mother is her telling me that *this* was going to be my wedding dress. I must've been three or four years old..." Lucy chewed on the bottom of her lip as she faced her reflection again. "I want to honor her today." Her palm smoothed over the bodice of the dress before she felt brave enough to face him head on. "Does it look alright?" It had been a long time since this dress saw the light of day, Lucy needed to make sure it wasn't stained or spotted somewhere she hadn't noticed.

"Lucy, you're beautiful." The words tumbled from Archie's lips before he could stop them. For years he'd tried to ignore the attraction between them, but it was getting harder by the second. In an attempt to keep those traitorous thoughts at bay, Archie turned his back. He noticed that her suitcase was sitting on the bed and he grabbed it without asking. "We should get going."

Lucy nodded her acquiescence. She did one last check to make sure she hadn't forgotten anything. She was ready as she'd ever be. After leaving a note for Danny, Lucy headed onto the porch. Her entire body tensed as Gabriel's arm snaked around her waist and he lifted her into his arms without warning. "What are you doing?" She gasped incredulously as Gabe carried her out to the van. "I'm pretty sure the tradition is to carry your bride over the threshold *into* the home, not out of it."

Archie smirked as he plopped her into the passenger seat. "It rained last night, Luce. I didn't want you to get any mud on your dress." He ignored the little voice in the back of his head telling him he was just looking for an excuse to hold her in his arms. Perhaps if he got used to Lucy in small doses, he could build up immunity once and for all. While his brain said that was a logical conclusion; his heart told him with every passing moment, he was in more danger of losing himself completely…never mind what his cock was thinking! That part of him was dying to skip the wedding and go straight for the honeymoon.

Lucy remained silent as they pulled out of the driveway and headed out to meet their fate. Most of Errol's citizens wouldn't begin to stir for several hours yet. The only two souls they saw on the drive through the neighborhood were the local paperboy and Old Man Jenkins who practiced yoga in his boxers every morning at dawn. Gabe's posture was tense and his knuckles were white from gripping the steering wheel. Lucy shifted uncomfortably in her seat. "Are you sure you want to do this."

"I'd give up my life for this club," Archie replied irritably. "I *am* giving my life up for this club," He muttered.

A flash of hurt clawed its way to the surface before Lucy could stop it. Anger filled her next but Lucy truly wasn't upset with Gabe, she was furious at *herself.* Of course he wouldn't want to marry her! He barely tolerated her. For the last ten years he'd gone out of his way to keep their interactions brief and curt. Getting married wasn't going to fix anything between them. Lucy tamped down on the impulse to drag her fingers through her curls; it would ruin her attempt to quell the frizz. She dug her fingernails into her palm instead. "It's not forever, Gabriel."

Archie visibly flinched. He *hated* being called Gabriel and Lucy knew it. There was only one woman who had ever called him by his Christian name and that was his mother. Lucy had long ago taken to calling him Gabriel when she was really angry or upset but Archie couldn't figure out why Lucy would be either right now. "If we're going to pull this off, we need to be honest with each other. So, you want to tell me why you're so pissed at me?"

"Where should I start?"

Sighing heavily, Archie eased into a spot in front of the tiny courthouse and killed the engine. "Look, I get it. You've got something to prove, Luce. You want in this club and you think that I'm standing in your way."

"You *are* standing in my way," Lucy countered. "When you found out Monster used your proxy to vote me in as a prospect, you threw the mother of all tantrums. Don't think I didn't notice the black eye he was sporting last night. I bet you put him on grunt work for the next six months, too." So far, Gabe was denying nothing. "*Then* you tried to intimidate me into giving up my patch and got pissed off when you failed. I'm not entirely convinced this wedding isn't your way of trying to control me!"

Archie pinched the bridge of his nose. "Excuse me for wanting to protect you! If you think these guys see you as anything but a pair of tits, you're out of your damn mind!" He snapped, "Most of them aren't like Danny and I. Many have criminal records, sexual deviances…some of them are even like my father."

Lucy felt her blood run cold. Gabe *never* talked about his father. The man who sired Gabriel was a member of the Wichita branch of the Devil's Own MC. Erik Archer was tall, dark, handsome, and a sociopath. He had a penchant for violence and served half a dozen years in prison for aggravated assault and battery. It all boiled down to the fact that Erik enjoyed knocking down those that were weaker than him; his favorite targets were his wife and young child. Gabriel was barely out of diapers when his mother had packed him up and sent him to Errol where the Hardings unofficially adopted him. To this day, Gabe still couldn't forget the bruises around his mother's throat or the tears in her eyes as she kissed him goodbye one last time. A week later, his mother shot Erik in the head moments before she succumbed to the injuries he inflicted on her. It was a tragedy Gabe had never truly recovered from…

Archie was vaguely aware Lucy had called his name several times. The soft touch of her hand against his shoulder startled him out of his memory. He wrenched away from her, his fist tightening on instinct. Archie's stomach tightened in agony when Lucy flinched. Why shouldn't she expect violence? Archie was convinced given half a chance, he would be the exact same kind of monster as Erik Archer was. Although his initial movement startled her, Lucy did not seem to be afraid. Her onyx eyes shimmered with a combination of empathy and annoyance. Archie furrowed his brows at her.

"Are you still with me?" Lucy's heart twisted in her chest as she watched him wrestle with invisible demons. She reached out again, refusing to be brushed aside this time.

Archie laid his palm over her hand for a brief moment, absorbing some of the strength she offered. Lucy was far too good for him; he had to keep reminding himself of that. "Let's just get this done. I want to be in Reno by noon." The moment Lucy stepped out of the van, sunshine beat down upon her ebony hair and illuminated her flawless skin. She looked like an angel. Guilt stabbed Archie in the gut as they trudged through the busted up parking lot at the courthouse. Lucy deserved a fairy tale wedding; she should walk down the aisle surrounded by friends and family into the arms of a man who would honor, protect, and cherish her for the rest of his life. This debacle wasn't even a close second.

Lucy remained quiet and level as she followed Gabe. Her eyebrow quirked up as she noticed her fellow prospects standing in front of the courthouse. Mort, Kyle, and Hunter were in various states of dishevelment, chatting quietly amongst themselves.

She stopped walking, folding her arms across her chest. "What are they doing here?"

Archie rested his hand at the small of her back to keep her moving. "We needed witnesses to make this legal. Besides, I figured if one prospect has to suffer, you should all have to." It was still very early; he'd had to call in a couple favors to get them in front of the judge first thing but it was worth it. The sooner they got this over with, the better.

Anita Raleigh looked up from her paperwork with a wide smile on her face. "When this came across my desk, I thought this was a prank. Lucy Harding getting married to Gabriel Archer. I never thought I'd see the day." Her crystal blue eyes sparkled with mirth. Anita was harmless and everyone knew it. She'd grown up two streets down from Lucy and they had been pretty good friends. Anita was a few years older than Lucy and one of the very few Errolites who'd actually gone to college. What was more impressive, she'd actually chosen a school out of state. Just like Anita's mother before her, she obtained her law degree and returned to her hometown where she'd practiced for a few months before being offered a judgeship. Errol had a longstanding history of 'keeping it in the family'. Everyone who lived here set down deep roots; some families, like Anita's, could trace their lineage back to the founding members of the town.

Lucy chuckled despite herself. "Yeah, well if you asked me about getting married yesterday, I'd probably have said you were insane." She ignored the look that Gabe shot her. "It took a while for this idiot to propose, but once he did, he was in a big damn hurry to make it legal." Gabe's expression tightened and Lucy resisted the urge to stick her tongue out at him.

"How romantic," Anita replied wistfully. There was not a single note of irony in her voice. "Well, let's get this show on the road, shall we?" Mort had taken it upon himself to explore the area, including Anita's personal pictures and her college diploma. She cleared her throat before she tugged away a photo of herself wearing a skimpy bikini while on spring break with her law school friends. "Today we come together to celebrate the union of Lucy Temperance Harding and Gabriel Stephen Archer."

Archie bit back a snicker. "I almost forgot your middle name was Temperance." He dodged the elbow aimed for his ribs. Lucy was anything but temperate, so her middle name was fantastically ironic.

Anita continued on, oblivious to the fact that Lucy and Archie were engaged in a silent battle of wills. "Marriage is a sacred union and is not to be entered into lightly. So before we begin, are there any objections or second thoughts?" Her eyes flicked between Lucy and Gabe. Neither of them moved and so she folded her hands, "Excellent. Have you prepared your own vows?"

"Yes," Archie sensed Lucy's shock and welcomed it. Everyone outside the club needed to believe this was real, starting with Anita. It just so happened he knew exactly how to sell it. "I remember the day we met like it was yesterday. I got off the plane with a flight attendant shepherding me to the pickup area. All I knew about your family was that my mother said you were good people." Archie had been only four at the time but he was wise beyond his years. "I didn't say a single word the whole way back to the house..." He vividly remembered being angry, scared, and fighting the urge to cry in front of everyone. "Then you reached out from your car seat and you held my hand. You were so small but somehow you knew exactly what I needed. I knew it was going to be okay." Archie squeezed her hands tighter in response. "So I stand in front of you today to promise you, *we* will be okay...I will be a good husband, one that you deserve. That's my solemn vow."

A loud sob drew attention away from the ceremony. Lucy thought it was Anita at first but quickly realized it was *Mort*. He grabbed tissues from a box on Anita's desk, whimpering after he loudly blew his nose. Lucy couldn't deny she felt a bit misty herself. She was barely a toddler when Gabe had come to live with them and hadn't realized how a simple gesture could mean so much to him. Or maybe was he just trumping it up to make it seem like they had an epic love connection. Either way, Gabe had definitely sold it.

Unfortunately, she had to come up with wedding vows that sounded just as intimate off the top of her head; it wasn't going to be easy. "Gabe, I've known you for almost my whole life. You were always made a great husband when we played house. Even though you preferred playing doctor, you always went along with what I wanted. I thank you for that…"

Hunter and Kyle both snickered. Anita let out a soft 'aww' at the sweetness of the moment. Mort cried louder. Archie could hardly bite back his groan. Why did she have to bring that up *now*?

Lucy continued mirthfully, "As we got older, I realized there was so much more to you than a companion and a playmate. You were my protector and my champion. I may not be the sweet, docile wife that you expected but I will do everything in my power to make you happy. That's my vow to you." Mort was wailing like a banshee now and Lucy felt confident she'd made it believable.

Archie reached into his pocket and pulled out a small box containing a ring that would put a robin's egg to shame. He slid it onto her finger, his hand lingering a moment as he watched Lucy's expression go from smug to shocked. The jeweler promised him that no woman could resist a set like this one and although it definitely put a dent in his life savings, Lucy deserved the best. Archie had also picked out a simple wedding band for himself. Lucy slipped it onto his finger with ease. The weight of it was odd but comfortable at the same time. Getting used to all of this would take time for both of them.

Anita smiled at the tender exchange between newlyweds. "By the power vested in me by the state of Nevada, I now pronounce you man and wife. You may kiss your bride." Anita bent over her desk to sign the marriage certificate with a flourish before passing it over to Kyle and Hunter to sign as witnesses; Mort was still whimpering and dabbing at his eyes. Thankfully, they only needed two signatures to make it legal.

Gabe and Lucy froze in the wake of Anita's words. Kissing wasn't mandatory, especially in a ceremony presided over by a judge...but it was out there and they couldn't very well ignore it. They would have to kiss or risk exposing their marriage as a sham. Given her propensity for town gossip, their plans could be over before they even began.

Gabe took a step forward and Lucy instinctively followed his lead. She held her breath as he bent down, his lips brushing over hers. The kiss was so gentle that at first she wasn't sure if she'd imagined it. He pulled away but the chaste peck on the lips didn't satisfy Lucy...she wanted more. Lucy threaded her fingers through his short hair and dragged him against her. Her body was instantly aflame when he sealed his lips over hers.

The feeling of Lucy's lush curves was enough to drive Archie over the edge. She was intoxicating. The taste of her favorite hazelnut coffee mingled with something that was wholly *Lucy*. He instinctively threaded his arms around her waist. He itched to undo the buttons on her wedding gown, reveal the creamy skin beneath and then continue his exploration much, *much* lower. A cacophony of coughing, courtesy of Kyle and Hunter, snapped Archie out of the moment. A minute longer and he would've gone too far...

Anita fanned herself exaggeratedly.
"Now *that's* what I call a kiss." She walked around her desk to give Lucy a congratulatory hug. "I get a lot of quickie marriages around here but I've never seen a couple who love each other as much as you two clearly do. I sincerely wish you the best of luck."

Lucy pasted a smile on and tried to ignore the heat simmering in her veins. "Thanks for your help, Anita." Lucy glanced over at where Kyle and Hunter were trying their best to comfort poor Mort. "And I'm really sorry about him..."

"I like a man who can express emotion." Anita's eyes swept over Mort appreciatively. She grabbed a tube of lipstick from the drawer and touched up her lips. Hunter and Kyle shared a look of disdain before hurrying out of the office without their crying comrade.

Shuddering, Lucy grabbed Gabe's hand. She didn't want to stick around to find out if Anita and Mort hit it off. "Come on, hubby, I think we've overstayed our welcome."

Archie followed Lucy blindly. He was still reeling from that kiss. He also had to shift several times so that no one would notice his primal reaction but thankfully, thinking about Anita and Mort getting it on was really helping. As soon as they were both buckled into the van, he pulled out onto the main road leading to the highway. It felt like centuries before they spoke again. "About the kiss—"

"We don't need to talk about it." Lucy still felt warm and tingly from *the kiss*. Anita's words weighed on her; she really thought Lucy and Gabe were in love. How preposterous was that? Lucy almost laughed. "The only thing that matters is Anita bought it. Kyle, Mort, and Hunter will inform a few strategic gossips in town and the news will be in Reno before we even arrive. Everything is falling into place. You should be happy."

Lucy was infuriating. Archie just wanted to make sure their soul-shattering lip lock hadn't made his new wife uncomfortable. Lucy refused to look him in the eye. He'd readily admit he didn't intend for his desire to run away with him like that. Maybe there was a part of him that wanted to know if she enjoyed it...but Lucy was content to freeze him out. Damn it all to hell, women were confusing! Archie aggressively merged onto the highway and headed for the city. He flicked the radio over to the rock station and settled in for a long drive. "We should be there in a couple hours."

"Sounds good. You need help navigating?" Lucy stifled a yawn.

"Nah, you should get some rest. I'll wake you when we get to the hotel." Gazing over at Lucy once more, Archie's anger died away as quickly as it flared up. She must have been tired because she went out like a light. The low music and the sound of her soft breathing were soothing as he zipped down toward the city. There was no telling what would be waiting for them in Reno…but for the moment, everything was calm.

Chapter Five

Lucy was in the middle of a slightly naughty dream when she was suddenly shaken awake. Wiping the corner of her mouth, she scrambled to sit up. She rubbed her scratchy eyes and looked around. Even though it was the middle of the afternoon, Reno's lights blinked and shone. There were hordes of people dressed to the nines; they walked up and down the sidewalks, stopping every once in a while to take pictures. Of what, exactly, Lucy wasn't sure. She was already overwhelmed and she hadn't even left the van. Pulling the visor down, Lucy groaned at her reflection. Her mascara had smudged, her dress was slightly rumpled, and her hair was sticking up in three different places. "Shit. Give me a minute to fix myself."

Archie chuckled and shrugged. Honestly, he thought Lucy looked adorable mussed from sleep. Her lips were swollen and softly parted; he longed to lean over and kiss them again. There was a certain softness about her right now that made him ache to hold her in his arms. Sarcasm was his only defense against her right now. "Take your time, princess. It's not like the future of our club is riding on this."

Lucy glared. "*Fine*, I'll walk into the hotel looking like a hungover raccoon. Who cares?" She pushed the car door open and reached for her suitcase but Gabe was faster. "I missed the part in our vows where you have to carry everything for me."

"Don't get your panties in a twist. It would be suspicious if I didn't dote on my new bride. Chivalry dictates I bring in your bags." When Lucy didn't protest he felt a sense of pride fill his chest. Archie actually won an argument and that was definitely worth celebrating. He was smiling from ear to ear as he ushered Lucy toward the lobby.

It was easily the swankiest place Lucy or Archie had ever been. A pair of tuxedoed doormen opened up the polished glass doors and ushered them into a giant atrium, complete with waterfall. The whole place was polished wood paneling from floor to ceiling, affixed with crystal chandeliers that caused speckled rainbows to reflect on the floor any time light hit them. The woman at the concierge desk looked like she'd been ripped from the pages of a fashion magazine. Her smile was bright and unwavering as Archie pulled the confirmations out of his pocket.

The model checking them in was giving Lucy a headache. The woman's voice was so high-pitched and squeaky, Lucy was sure there were dogs barking all over Reno. The attendant was halfway through a spiel about some of the amenities in the brochure when Lucy interrupted. "I don't think we're going to be partaking of any spa services this trip." Plucking the room keys from the clerk's hand, Lucy flashed the girl a winning smile. "You mind if we get to the room? I'm itching to get my new husband out of his jeans." If the girl minded, it certainly didn't show on her face. Gabriel, on the other hand, looked like he was about to swallow his tongue.

"Right this way, Mrs. Archer."

The honeymoon suite was on the top floor, overlooking the entire city. Perfectly crafted French doors were the gateway into a massive room. Straight ahead was a balcony that housed a heart-shaped hot tub. The bed was on a platform with two steps and tucked between white Doric columns; delicate red rose petals had been sprinkled over it. There were his and hers armoires on either side of the room, nestled a dresser. A television was mounted on the wall, boasting six hundred channels and pay per view movies. Just beyond that, a simple door led to a sleek black marble bathroom with a whirlpool tub and steam shower. Champagne and strawberries were settled on a bar cart along with handwritten, heartfelt congratulations from the staff of the Paradise Resort and Spa. The entire place exuded luxury and privilege.

Gabriel had clearly spent a fortune on a honeymoon that meant nothing. Lucy was shocked, but not disappointed. Although she was dying to explore, she started to unpack. First things first, she needed to hang her wedding gown very carefully. If she were ever blessed with a daughter of her own, the dress would belong to her...if not, Danny was bound to knock someone up sooner or later. *His* daughter could have it. Either way, Lucy would allow no harm to come to the family heirloom. "Hey Casanova, can you help me with these buttons again?"

Archie couldn't tear his eyes away from Lucy. Now that they were truly alone, he was going to have a hard time controlling his baser impulses. He tamped down on his lust and closed the distance between them. While she swept away several dark curls that had escaped the pins, he tried to brush aside the wicked thoughts that bombarded him. He longed to pull the rest of the pins and drag his fingers through her hair as he kissed down the sensitive contour of her neck...

Releasing the buttons as quickly as possible, Archie tried to ignore the creamy skin that he unearthed as he went. He had to steel himself against leaning in to taste that unexplored terrain. After several minutes of exquisite torture, Archie heaved a sigh of relief. "There you go." Archie: 1. Libido: 0.

"Thanks," Lucy held her dress against her chest as she padded toward the bathroom. "So what's first? I'm sure you have a whole plan mapped out on how to win over this territory."

"You don't want to start with tearing me out of my jeans?" Archie grinned, stuffing his hands into his pockets. He was feeling a little cocky now that he'd managed not to succumb to his desire for her.

Lucy turned a little too quickly and the dress slipped, revealing more of her lacy white bra. "I didn't need the thirty minute explanation of services, Gabe. You wanted us to act like a newlywed couple. I think two people who love each other and were recently married would be very eager to get to the room and consummate the union."

"Jesus Christ, Lucy!" All the annoyance that gnawed at Archie suddenly died away. Lucy made it easier to forget she was gorgeous by hiding her curves with baggy t-shirts and jeans but she had such a luscious body hiding beneath. It was all he could do not to ravage her.

"Oh come on, it's not like you've never seen a woman naked before!" Lucy's face scorched with embarrassment. She fled to the bathroom to avoid the hungry look in Gabe's eyes. Lucy changed into a cutoff pair of shorts and a Harley Davidson t-shirt that she practically swam in. It was the most unflattering outfit in her repertoire. For good measure, Lucy took her time heading back into the room. She splashed a bit of water on her face to remove her makeup and she pulled the pins from her hair. When she returned, he was still standing where she'd left him with a dumbfounded expression on his face.

Lucy carried the dress to the armoire and hung it on a velvet hanger. Gabe was an enigma to her. Obviously, he'd dragged his hand through his hair several times and it was gently mussed. The barest hint of a five o'clock shadow darkened his chiseled jawline. Lucy kept reminding herself this was a professional arrangement, not a personal one. It was better to keep things as businesslike as possible. "Earth to Gabe? I need to know what the plan is."

Archie cleared his throat several times. "Right. We need to lay low for a couple days. You hit the nail on the head before: newlywed couples don't immediately hit the town the day after the wedding." Unfortunately, he wasn't sure how he'd survive several days holed up with Lucy. The room suddenly seemed too small. "We'll use that time to strategize. I have a meeting set up with an ex-Jack. He's willing to help us figure out the Black Jack's strategy for keeping a hold on the city. Plus there are a couple potential prospects that might be interested in pledging their loyalty to the Devil's Own. But for now, we bide our time."

Lucy flopped onto the bed, tucking her legs beneath her, "A few *days*? What the hell are we going to do? Stare at each other?"

Archie shrugged. "We could start with some room service. I figure you must be hungry." A smirk slid over his features as he thumbed through the expensive room service menu. "I forgot to tell you the best part. This entire honeymoon is on Monster's dime. It's part of his punishment. It was Danny's idea. So, get whatever you want, sweetheart. It's not costing me a thing."

Annoyance seared through Lucy as she stared Gabe down. Did he really think she was going to be happy that Monster was being punished for helping her? Lucy rolled her eyes. "Why don't you pop that champagne too? It's my wedding day and I want to be toasted, one way or another." Maybe it would take the edge off. Lucy clinked her crystal champagne flute against Gabe's. "Here's to a short marriage with the least amount of awkwardness."

"I'll drink to that." Archie drained his champagne in one long sip. "It's not half bad…" While Lucy placed an order for an obscenely large amount of food, he settled down on the bed beside her. Although the room was large, it was created for newlywed couples and that would make sleeping arrangements very difficult. "There's only one bed," Archie observed.

Lucy's lips quirked upward into a smile. "I'm sure you'll be very comfortable in the tub or on the sofa over there."

"I'm taller than you. I won't fit on that tiny couch!" Archie refilled their glasses and drained a second one before he spoke again. The alcohol was already starting to cloud Archie's judgment. "You know, it wouldn't be the first time we shared a bed."

Lucy chuckled, "If you hadn't noticed, I'm not five years old anymore."

Archie's eyes swept over her figure appreciatively. "I noticed."

It wasn't as if he could see through her oversized t-shirt but somehow Lucy felt as if he could. She scoffed and pulled the menu tight against her chest for good measure. "Ha, ha," She grunted, sarcastically. "The answer is still no." Skittering away from him, Lucy was desperate for a subject change. "How come there aren't any prices on anything?"

"Probably because you wouldn't buy it if you knew how expensive it was." Archie smirked at the incredulity on her face. "Don't worry about it, Luce. This is our honeymoon. You should enjoy yourself."

Lucy traced the rim of her champagne flute with her finger guiltily. In Errol, there weren't any fancy places like this around. Right off the main drag there was a motor lodge that was reserved for passersby or philandering spouses. The small town also boasted a bed and breakfast where *everybody* went for romantic getaways. Although the B&B was charming, it didn't hold a candle to the fancy honeymoon suite they found themselves in now. Lucy had to say, she didn't mind the lap of luxury.

Archie itched to run his fingers through the dark hair had come loose from Lucy's ponytail. There was a warm bloom of pink in her cheeks that accentuated her beauty. He couldn't stop staring at her rosebud lips. His mind kept wandering back to Anita's office and the electric shock of pleasure that burned through him when Lucy's lips met his. Archie knew his way around women; he enjoyed sex and wasn't afraid to admit it...but in his entire life, he had never been so enticed by one single kiss.

"You're staring at me." Lucy shifted uncomfortably.

Archie startled. *Busted*. "No I wasn't," He lied baldly.

Lucy rolled her eyes. "We're going to be stuck in this room together for two days—"

"Three."

Lucy huffed at this interruption. "*Three* days." She crossed her legs, facing him head on. "Don't you think it would be great to spend that time doing something productive? We could talk about club business or put an *actual* plan in place for taking Reno back from the Black Jacks?"

"You're not a Devil yet, Lucy. You know damn well I can't discuss club business with you," Archie frowned. Leave it to Lucy to try and weasel her way around the rules.

"I am your *only* backup out here," Lucy shot back. "If we want to survive, you can't keep me in the dark. I need to know who we're meeting with and what the danger is." She gazed deep into his cobalt eyes, unflinchingly. "You told me your only goal is to keep me safe, Gabe. What's safe about going into this blind?"

Archie gritted his teeth and dragged his fingers through his hair again. Damn it...Lucy was right. "Anything I tell you is on a need to know basis *and* you can't let anyone in the MC know what I've told you. I won't have my authority questioned." There was always someone waiting in the wings to try and win the Presidency. Archie won the vote fair and square several years running but the position was certainly coveted. Since their inception, The Devils Own MC had seen dictators rise and fall. No one wanted a repeat of the bloodshed and violence ten years ago when they lost half their territory— and their crew—to the Black Jacks.

Lucy nodded eagerly. "That's all I'm asking, Gabe. I have your back no matter what, I just need you to have mine." What they were going into was extremely dangerous. The Black Jacks were ruthless; he would need her by his side if they were going to take them down.

"I would never let anything happen to you." The very thought of Lucy getting hurt was like a hot iron to Archie's heart.

Lucy folded her arms tightly over her chest. "I think you forget sometimes that I'm not a little girl. Maybe you'd have gotten it through your thick skull by now if you actually talked to me once in a while." Lucy never told Gabe how badly it hurt her when he suddenly stopped being her friend. He used to let her ride on the back of his motorcycle and take her mini-golfing or to the movies; sometimes they wouldn't go anywhere at all and make a bonfire in the backyard. Although she spent the summer of her sixteenth birthday in Oakland, she eagerly anticipated coming home to Gabe again. When he suddenly couldn't even look at her anymore, it cut deep. "I really don't know what it is I did to piss you off but for the sake of this club, I need you to put it aside."

Archie furrowed his eyebrows, "What are you talking about? I'm not pissed off at you, Lucy."

"Oh yeah?" Lucy countered. "I can't even count how many of my phone calls you've dodged or how many parties you've left because I was there. You've been going out of your way to avoid me for years and…I don't know why."

A cold sweat broke out over Archie's back. He stood up off the bed, towering over her as he did so. Lucy wasn't wrong; he kept her at arm's length but he had to in order to protect both of them. "This is ridiculous. Just forget it."

"I'm not going to forget it," Lucy pressed. "You said you wanted honesty, Gabriel. Now it's time to put your money where your mouth is." Lucy refused to back down. "You can barely look at me. You don't come for the holidays anymore, even though Danny and I are the only family you have." A decade of unresolved issues boiled over suddenly. "There's still a room for you at our place even though you choose to sleep at the club every night. I know it was hard for you when my parents died, Gabe. I know you loved them too…but this started long before that. I want to know why."

Anger welled in Archie's gut. He did love the Hardings; they took him in and molded him into the man he was today. But he also loved Lucy…and it was *definitely* not in the way a brother was supposed to love a sister. The harder Lucy pushed, the harder it was for Archie to continue lying to himself. "It's not that simple!"

Lucy cried in exasperation, "*What's* not simple?"

"I'm attracted to you!" Archie thundered, his cheeks burning red. The truth was out in the open now.

There was no going back. His stomach twisted into knots as he waited for her to respond.

There was a beat of silence before Lucy rocked back on her heels. "*So*?" She felt the exact same way about him. How could anyone *not* be attracted to Gabe? He was the fantasy of every woman in Washoe County...maybe even the world. "You mean to tell me you've been avoiding me for ten years because you've got a crush on me?" Lucy snapped. "For Christ's sake, Gabriel, that's the stupidest thing I've ever heard!"

Well, it made sense at the time, Archie thought to himself. He turned away from Lucy only to find her in his face again. He rebuffed her, putting even more distance between them. "Cut it out!"

Lucy shook her head fiercely. "You don't avoid someone you care about because of a little sexual tension! I thought I'd done something wrong, Gabe. I thought maybe I hurt you somehow..."

Archie did hurt...he came from a long line of drunks, junkies, and abusers. The Archers were the scum of the earth and no one felt that more acutely than he did. Lucy was incredible. One day she would be loved by a man who would worship the ground she walked on; she would have children with a man who adored them all. Archie wouldn't give her those things...his blood was a curse. He was destined to become the same kind of scumbag his father was. If he let Lucy get closer, if he gave in just a little bit, he would never be strong enough to leave her. The cycle had to stop somewhere and Archie was determined it would be with him.

Archie turned his back, icing her out yet again. "I'm done with this conversation, Lucy." The heavy knock of room service was a welcome relief from the heated argument they were having. He answered the door gruffly, but tipped well enough to make up for his sour attitude. His appetite was spoiled now but he sat down at the table anyway, stabbing at the steak he'd ordered.

Lucy grabbed her plate and plopped down across from him. Heavy silence hung between them, causing the tension to rise even further. Grabbing the remote, Lucy flicked through six hundred channels of nothing. "Saved by the Bell?" Archie didn't look amused. She rolled her eyes pointed at the television mounted on the wall. "Do you want to watch it or not?"

"You're purposely trying to provoke me." Archie grabbed the bottle of champagne, fully intending to drown away his sorrows. He poured them both another glass and pounded it down.

They ate in silence, avoiding each other's gazes. Lucy tried to focus on the television but
the uneasiness between them was too much of a distraction. Finally, she was unable to hold back her ire a moment longer. "You know what I think?" Gabe opened his mouth to cut her off but Lucy was faster.

"I think you've overestimated what you feel for me. It's just a teenage crush. We just need to get past this and I think the best way to do that is to get it all out of your system."

Archie mulled over Lucy's words, searching for meaning but coming up empty. Food forgotten, he peered at her levelly. "How the hell do you propose we do that?"

"I think we should have sex."

The champagne flute in Archie's hand went flying, spilling its contents all over the table before it crashed onto the floor. "Are you out of your mind?"

"Come on, think about it!" Lucy pressed. "Half the time when you get something you really want, it doesn't live up to your expectations. The novelty wears off and you move on. What's between us is no different..." Or so she thought. "We have three days in this stupid hotel room. I bet by then you'll be satisfied and ready to move on. Then we can pretend like none of this happened and focus on the club." Lucy paused. "Besides, we're *married*. It's basically our job to do it." There was a part of Lucy that was dying to know what it would be like to take him to bed. She, too, had nursed a crush on Gabe for far more years than she cared to admit. This would satisfy her curiosity, cut the tension, and Lucy had no doubt it would be incredibly fun.

Archie tried to come up with a viable argument against her proposal while he mopped up champagne…but he couldn't think of a single reason. Maybe he *had* grown infatuated over the years. Maybe his raging desire for her only affected him because he'd denied himself for so long. Things would certainly be easier if he could clarify the situation and his feelings for Lucy. After a long internal debate, Archie sighed in defeat. "You're serious about this?"

Lucy grinned triumphantly. She'd already won. "I think we *have* to do this, for both our sakes."

"Well, when you put it that way…" Archie closed the distance between them. In one fell swoop, he dragged Lucy out of her chair and wrapped her tightly in his arms. The gasp of pleasure that tore from her throat sent shivers down his spine. Archie plundered her mouth, reliving every exquisite moment of this morning's kiss as he eagerly free her dark hair from its tie. He tangled his fingers in the silky strands, wild curls spilling over her shoulders and framing her face. Archie's blood sang in his veins, thundering through his body and pumping to fill the aching length of him.

Lucy had only been with one man in her life, a stupid mistake she'd made when she was nineteen. She thought the sex between them was good at the time…she had no problem admitting she was wrong. Wrapped in Gabriel's tight embrace now, Lucy had never been so impassioned. Flames erupted in her core, slowly melting the iciness inside her. Her nipples tightened as they dragged against the hard plane of his chest. They were suddenly heavy and aching for his touch. Eagerly, she pressed against him, marveling at how he could be so thickly muscled and yet so tender at the same time. Lucy's fingertips teased down his sides until she reached the waistband of his jeans.

Archie was already teetering on the brink of insanity. He'd never noticed how intoxicating the faint smell of lavender and lilac was mixed with the clean scent of her skin. When her hand snuck closer to his aching manhood, he was lost. Sweeping Lucy into his arms, Archie carried her to the bed. He pressed soft kisses to her lips before dipping lower. Pushing the oversized t-shirt up over her head, he couldn't stop the hungry growl that emanated from his throat as the lace cups of her bra were once again within his sight.

Panting softly at the overwhelming rush of pleasure, Lucy's fingernails trailed over Gabriel's warm skin. He gazed at her like he was a wolf and she his prey, ready be devoured. Lucy arched against the roughness of his fingers on her newly naked flesh. Gabe must have read her mind as he dipped down, releasing one breast from her bra and sucking the hard bud of her nipple into his mouth. Lucy's onyx eyes fluttered closed as he lavished his attention over sensitive skin. She was positive his only goal was to drive her mad with pleasure.

Archie was blown away at how infinitely responsive Lucy was to him. Every moan and whimper spurned him onward. Once he got his fill of her breasts, he kissed down the soft curve of her waist. He popped open the button on her denim shorts as he went. Archie teased the fabric down her hips, taking a moment to drink in the sight of her writhing in ecstasy. Lucy was the most beautiful woman he'd ever seen…and she was *all* his.

It seemed wholly unfair that Lucy was bare while Gabe was still fully clothed. He reached for her again but she clucked her tongue, "Your turn." Tearing at the fabric of his shirt, she grinned darkly at the muted sound of buttons cascading onto the floor. Next, she eased down the zipper on his jeans achingly slowly, pressing her fingertips into his hips as she uncovered his turgid length. Gabriel Archer was a god among men. Muscles bulged and glistened with a light sheen of sweat as their primal dance picked up pace. His eyes shimmered with need, mirroring her own desperation to take him inside her. Lucy yearned to reach out and explore every exquisite detail of Gabe's body; but there would be time for that later. Right now, they both needed release.

Lucy's fingers tangled in his hair as she kissed him again. She used the vantage point to tug him between her legs. It was all the encouragement he needed. With infinite care, Archie pressed Lucy against the mattress. Her nails scraped down his back as he slipped between her legs, pausing at her entrance. "Are you ready?" He ground out.

"Yes." Lucy threw her head back, drawing in a ragged breath as Gabe finally filled her. Pleasure coursed through every cell in her body, launching her into a higher plane of existence. She was lost to him and he hadn't even begun to move yet. The first stroke dragged a cry from her throat as she clung to him for dear life.

It took every ounce of strength in Archie's body not to lose control right then and there. Lucy was warm, wet, and willing in his arms. She accepted him so wholly that he nearly wept with the pleasure of it. Kissing her brutally, Archie arched his back to press deeper into the heart of her. Her soft cries of pleasure only fueled his desire and he rewarded her by increasing the pace. Lucy's nails sunk into his flesh and he groaned; the pain-pleasure of her clawing his back was all he could bear. Without hesitation, without fear, Archie unleashed ten years of pent up frustration and need into her womb.

Lucy rode wave after wave of orgasmic pleasure as Gabe treated her to the most intense release of her life. Every touch, every stroke, every breath was meant to drive her beyond the brink of human experience. There was such blessed relief as his warmth curled in her belly. It was the singular most beautiful moment of her life.

For several minutes after, Archie remained joined with Lucy. His eyes were firmly shut and he knew without a doubt this marriage had been a mistake. Making love to Lucy tore something open inside him. He couldn't risk falling in love with her anymore than he already had. But now that he had a taste, he wasn't sure he could stop. Archie rested his head against her shoulder, occasionally pressing soft kisses to her warm flesh. "Well, that was a miserable failure..." He murmured. "You are not out of my system."

Lucy chuckled throatily. "Beginner's luck?" Her fingertips traced over his bicep. "I think we should keep at it. The novelty will wear off eventually, right?" Or maybe it wouldn't. Either way, Lucy was deliciously sated right now and she wasn't ready to let that feeling go just yet.

"Mmm..." Archie replied, "I guess we'll have to wait and see." Pressing a soft kiss to her lips, he finally disentangled himself. "*After* we eat. I'm suddenly starving." Archie was glad they'd ordered plenty of room service.

"Me too," Lucy laughed and grabbed a robe from the armoire. She tossed him one before settling down at the table. Things were comfortable again. Lucy and Archie laughed at some stupid sitcom on television, ate their tepid meals, and finished off the rest of the champagne before falling into bed again. Before the night was through, they made love twice more. Exhaustion eventually won out and they both fell into a deep sleep, happily tangled in each other's arms. It was bliss.

Chapter Six

Three days sounded like such a long time at first, and yet Lucy marveled at how quickly they passed while she was wrapped in Gabe's arms. Their first meeting of the day was set for noon, which should have been sufficient time to get up and out of the hotel, if they hadn't been up all night...

When the alarm went off, Lucy warred against her instincts and forced herself to get out of bed. Gabe must have sensed her disdain because he joined her in the shower and spent their remaining time alone making love against the cool marble tile. If there was any question of Gabe and Lucy being newlyweds it was most certainly dispelled when they hurried into the dingy bar wet, disheveled, and murmuring apologies for their tardiness.

Peter "Pip" Reardon had been a member of the Black Jacks since he was eighteen years old. In his youth he might have been handsome, but now he was wizened and gray. His hands were gnarled from holding onto the handlebars of his bike for so long. Not to mention his skin and teeth were yellowed from years of drinking and smoking. Pip's anger at the Black Jacks stemmed from the fact they had stripped him of his patch. After a minor stroke in his seventies, he wasn't allowed to ride with them anymore and, eventually, became obsolete. An orderly guided Pip's wheelchair to the table. Bitterness exuded out of his every pore. "There's no respect anymore. I dedicated my life to the Black Jacks and they screwed me over!" Pip's voice was raspy and harsh. Even talking made him short of breath and he descended into a terrible wheezing cough.

Lucy watched Pip with concern as he struggled to breathe. "I'll be right back. I'm going to get you some water," She offered. Despite being in the throes of hacking, Pip smiled. Lucy's fingertips slid over Gabe's shoulder as she headed toward the bar.

"Girls like that don't come around too often. Hang onto her," Pip managed to squeak out between coughs. Grabbing his oxygen tank from beneath the table, he tugged the mask over his face and inhaled deeply. "Ah, that's the stuff..." He murmured. Although his words were still punctuated by labored spurts of breath, Pip regained his bearings for the moment. "Let's get down to business. I've got dialysis in an hour."

Archie pinched the bridge of his nose to stem the throbbing of annoyance creeping toward his brain. He never expected Pip Reardon to be so frail. Archie remembered hearing stories about how fierce Pip had been back in the day. It also didn't help the old fool's case that he stared at Lucy lewdly. Pip's wrinkled hand lingered over hers as he accepted the cup of water. The possessiveness that rose up in Archie was wholly unpleasant. He had always been driven to protect Lucy but now rage speared through him if anyone so much as looked at her sideways. Jealousy was not a good look on him. Archie cleared his throat loudly. "So, you told me there has been a shift of power? A new leader who's changing the way the club works?" The things Pip had told him were terrifying, to say the least. The sooner Archie was able to stop the Black Jacks, the better.

Pip took a long drink of his water before he nodded. "When Sal took over, everything changed. The Black Jacks used to be about glory! We were feared and respected...and we could take down anyone who got in our way. All this dumb bitch wants to do is deal cards and call in loans. There's this compound built out in the desert where they got a whole army a' people locked up for safe keepin' but I kept tellin' 'em they ain't worth nothin'! The Black Jacks are better than that!"

Disgust churned in Lucy's veins as she listened to Pip bemoan the fact that there had been a decrease in violence and raids since 'Sal' took over. It was that kind of violence that got her parents gunned down in the street without mercy. Pip could've been the one who killed her parents. He certainly seemed to enjoy boasting about his bloody triumphs.

Archie could feel the anger radiating off Lucy in waves while Pip was rambling on about his glory days. Archie reached over, grasping her hand tightly. As respectfully as he could manage, Gabe cut off

Pip's longwinded story about shooting up a strip club. "What can you tell us about where the Black Jacks operate? They must have a setup somewhere in the city."

"You ever heard of the Aces High?" Pip leaned in. "It's a crumbling piece of crap casino on North Virginia Street. Place has been bought and foreclosed three times in the last fifty years but Sal refuses to let go. Says there's charm in the old place!" He snorted disdainfully, "Sentimental bitch…"

Archie furrowed his eyebrows. "What kind of security have they got?"

"The usual stuff, security guards, guns in the back, cameras." Pip shrugged, "But anybody can walk in there. It's a workin' casino. They've got a few slots that are rigged to lose." Pip folded his hands on the table. "Everybody knows you go to the Ace if you want to play cards. Sal will take a bet on anything, whether it's the deed to your house or a rare parakeet. No other casino within a hundred miles of here takes those kind of bets."

"So people bet whatever they have and Sal cheats them out of their livelihood?" Lucy frowned markedly. During prohibition, the Devil's Own had earned their reputation by moving illegal booze countrywide. When the law was repealed, the Devils branched out into auto parts and stolen cars. These days, they made their money doing legitimate repairs on bikes and cars, plus had a side business running the bar at the clubhouse. Other branches of the Devil's Own were still notorious for their crime but in Errol, the novelty wore off long ago.

Pip snorted derisively. "That's the worst part. We've been sayin' for years to stack the deck. Easiest way to make money! But Sal says business will die off if people smell cheatin' at cards. It's bullshit if you ask me…" He cursed bitterly until he dissolved into yet another fit of coughing.

Archie was sick of listening to this doddering old fool. He wasn't telling them anything worth their time. Standing abruptly, Archie pulled an envelope with a few hundred dollars in it and threw it down on the table. "We appreciate your help." He managed a gruff goodbye before grasping Lucy's hand and pulling her out of the bar and away from that horrible man. Lucy said nothing as they headed down the sidewalk toward their hotel. The smell of cinnamon and freshly baked bread wafted in front of him and Archie realized they hadn't stopped to eat anything yet today. "Come on, I'll buy you breakfast."

"I'm not really hungry," Lucy shrugged. "But I could use a cup of coffee. There's a café up ahead." The aroma of freshly ground coffee beans fortified her as they stepped over the threshold. Gabe stood so close that his chest kept bumping against her back. Usually, Lucy would find a gesture like that to be overbearing but given the fact they had the most amazing sex of her life, all awkwardness was gone.

Archie couldn't keep his eyes off Lucy. She seemed a little off kilter since the meeting with Pip. "Are you alright? You seem a little flushed," He pressed. These last three days had not exactly had the effect that he'd been hoping for. Archie was still waiting for the part where he stopped craving her like she was a drug…

"I'm fine," Lucy brushed off his concern. She ordered herself a hazelnut latte and, at Archie's behest, grabbed a croissant from the display case. Padding over to a booth near the back, she smiled as he sat across from her with a large black coffee in hand. "So, was the meeting everything you hoped?"

Archie tore a piece off Lucy's croissant and popped it into his mouth. "Some of it was helpful. I think our first step is to check out that casino." He smirked. "Danny told me you used to clean up at the card tables."

"Mom loved cards. She taught me how to play hearts, blackjack, and poker." Lucy smiled nostalgically at the memory. "When mom and I would visit the family in California the days were filled with swimming, touring vineyards, and sightseeing but every night we'd sit around on the patio and play for hours." Inexplicably, tears built behind Lucy's dark eyes.

Archie was shocked by her sudden display of emotion and reached out instinctively to comfort her. "Luce…" It tore a hole in his chest seeing how distraught she was. He suddenly felt like the most callous jerk who'd ever lived. "I didn't stop to think about how hard this was going to be for you. I'm sorry." Archie's thumb stroked over the back of her hand. "I know you miss your parents. Especially your mom…" There was no mother and daughter closer than Lucy and Louisa Harding.

Lucy's attempts to rein in her emotion became futile. A sob escaped her throat and she covered her face, desperate not to let him see her crumble. Anger quickly replaced her grief but it did nothing to stem the flow of tears. If anything, her rage deepened the chasm of hurt swirling inside her. Lucy didn't want to cry in front of anyone, let alone Gabriel and the patrons of this little cafe. "I can't believe I'm doing this *now*."

Something broke inside Archie. He stood and moved to her side of the booth, wrapping his arms around her. For once, Lucy didn't fight him. She allowed him to hold her in his strong embrace. He pressed a tender kiss to the top of her head and cradled her tighter. "It's okay, let it out," He murmured softly.

Burying her face in Gabe's shoulder, Lucy felt as if ten years of pent up frustration and tears poured out of her. He rubbed her back and murmured soft words of comfort in her ear. For the longest time, Lucy allowed him to simply hold her until the tightness eased from her throat. Lucy grabbed a napkin and dabbed at her eyes before she turned away again. "I'm so embarrassed," She whispered, her voice hoarse with emotion.

"Why?" Archie furrowed his eyebrows. He cupped her cheek, brushing away a stray tear. "It's okay to be vulnerable sometimes."

"I just had a meltdown in public over *nothing*." Lucy scoffed, shaking her head. She turned away from Gabe and took a long sip of her latte. It was tepid now, but the caffeine was very welcome.

"Losing your parents isn't nothing, Lucy. I can see how listening to Pip recount war stories of destruction and violence during his years as a Black Jack could dredge some things up." The icy façade she put up to keep everyone out was cracking and he was in awe of the woman beneath. Lucy had been so strong for so long; how she managed it, he wasn't sure. "You went from being a teenage girl with two parents to having to raise Danny all by yourself."

A sharp bark of laughter emanated from Lucy's throat before she could stop it. No one had ever acknowledged that before. Everyone commended Danny for taking custody of his little sister and raising her in their parents' absence. But the truth of the matter was it was Lucy who kept Danny from self-destructing, even after all these years. She smiled blearily, "You caught that one, did you?"

Archie shot her a sympathetic grin. "Danny's got a lot of great qualities but responsibility has never been one of them." He sighed heavily, "I think that's why he goes home with a different girl every night. He wants the physical comfort of being with someone but doesn't want to open himself up to getting hurt."

"Whoa," Lucy raised an eyebrow. "When did you become Dr. Phil?"

Archie scrubbed a hand over his stubbled chin. Lucy shared a lot about herself today and he decided it was time to return the favor. After all, he had promised her honesty…it was time to hold up his end of the deal. "Do you remember when we were kids? On Thursdays, your mom and I used to drive into Sun Valley." Curling his hands tighter around his cup of coffee, he gritted his teeth.

"Yeah, that was the night you went to karate," Lucy replied blandly. Where was this going?

"I don't know karate, Lucy…" Archie nervously picked at the Styrofoam cup. "I was four years old when I came to live with your family. At first, I was a wreck. I wouldn't eat, I couldn't sleep." He let out a shaky breath, "The doctor recommended I see a psychiatrist." Every word of his confession was like tearing up a wound stitch by stitch. Archie shifted uncomfortably, "I started seeing someone every week. Slowly but surely, things started to improve." He licked his lips. "Your mother thought it might be embarrassing for me to admit that I was in therapy so she fibbed about where we went. For the longest time, I *did* feel ashamed. Maybe I still do? I've never admitted this to a single person, Lucy...except for you."

A feeling of warmth spread over her as she gazed at Gabe. The fact that he trusted her enough with something so personal made her heart soar. "You're the bravest person I know." Lucy knew all too well that Gabe and his mother had been abused by his father. "What you went through as a kid was awful. I can't imagine what it would be like to be hurt by someone who's supposed to love you unconditionally." She saw Gabe's jaw tighten and, this time, she reached for him, "Do you still go?"

"Not since high school. Hopefully thirteen years of therapy was enough." Archie was on solid ground now and felt as if he'd worked through his issues with his father. Still, there was a niggling voice at the back of his head that told him he was still bad and he'd turn into an abusive monster eventually. It was better to keep Lucy at arm's length than to fall into the same cycle as the rest of the men in his family.

Lucy nodded slowly. She took a long swig of coffee, memorizing the expression on Gabe's face. He was so handsome that sometimes she didn't look past his sharp features and shimmering cobalt eyes, but there was so much more to him. His features tightened when he was angry, his eyebrows furrowed and his nostrils flared. When he was sad,

73

there was slackness to his jaw and a slight downturn of his lips—that was the expression he was wearing today. Lucy ached to kiss him until that sultry look of joy and satisfaction was the only one they remembered. A change in subject seemed necessary. "Do we have any other meetings today?"

"Nope, I didn't want to draw any unnecessary attention. Too many people coming in and out would tip the Black Jacks off." Archie replied. "But in light of this new information, I was thinking we should get dressed up and hit the card tables. It'll be a good way to gather intel. Hey, maybe we'll even make a few bucks."

"Let's not get carried away," Lucy teased, grabbing her coffee and wrapping the half-eaten croissant in a napkin for later. She found herself glancing over at Gabe as they walked back toward the hotel. His hand slid around her waist, comforting her immensely. Lucy found herself wondering if this little gesture was part of the act or if he just wanted to touch her? She didn't have the courage to ask...

Housekeeping had come and gone while they were out, the room once again put back in pristine condition. Lucy plopped down on the bed and watched Gabe hawkishly. "When you said you wanted to dress, you meant a pair of nice jeans and a shirt, right?"

Archie furrowed his eyebrows, "You have a dress, don't you?"

"Well, I have my wedding dress…" Lucy frowned. Opening up the closet, Archie unzipped the garment bag. Inside was a charcoal gray three-piece suit he'd picked up off the rack a couple weeks ago. Her mouth dropped open. "You mean to tell me you wore jeans to our wedding when you had *that* with you all along?"

"I thought you said I looked good!" Archie bristled, folding his arms over his chest.

He *had* looked good. Lucy wouldn't have changed a single thing about their wedding but this news still made her stop and think. "Never mind…" She dug through the clothes that remained in her bag. "I seriously have nothing to wear." Tugging t-shirts out, she laid them on the bed. One of her tank tops had rhinestones around the neckline and she did have that one dusty skirt—but that was about the extent of her 'fancy' clothing.

Archie dug through the clothes and shook his head curtly. "This won't do." He frowned. "We'll just have to go shopping." For any of the other women he knew, that decree would elicit joy. Lucy, on the other hand, groaned as if he told her he was going to waterboard her. "Hey, I don't like it either, sweetheart."

Lucy wanted to be angry but when Gabe stepped out in his suit, she forgot to be. She smiled appreciatively as he went from rugged biker to sharp-dressed hunk. Her heart fluttered in her chest at how badly she wanted him right now. "You clean up nice…"

"I'll look forward to getting dirty again later," Archie chuckled, closing the distance between them. He pressed a gentle kiss to her lips. "Now, come on. We need to get you something to wear that'll blow everyone's mind. The Black Jacks won't be expecting us to walk through the door of their hideout in our Sunday best."

"Sure, that makes sense." Lucy genuinely wished they could get dirty again *now*. She decided to keep that musing to herself as they headed downstairs to grab directions to the nearest shopping plaza. According to the shrill-voiced clerk who'd checked them in yesterday there was a plaza on South Virginia Street, just a little ways down from the casinos.

To avoid detection and keep their cover intact, Archie got them a cab. The less people knew of their whereabouts, the safer they'd be. He gazed over at her as they headed down the bustling Reno streets. "I want to make sure you call me Gabriel whenever we're in public…"

Lucy's expression changed to one of surprise. "You *hate* it when I call you by your full name!"

"I knew it! I *knew* you used my name to punish me," Archie scoffed. He shook his head in annoyance.

"Even our enemies call me Archie. There are very few people who know my actual name and that works out to our advantage. You call me by my real name and nobody will be any the wiser." He narrowed his eyes. "A slip up could make us targets."

"You don't need to worry. I never liked your stupid nickname anyway," Lucy sighed heavily. "Gabriel is a beautiful name. It means strength and wisdom. It's perfect for you."

Archie always thought she called him Gabe just to annoy him; knowing there was more to the story felt like a punch to his gut. Staring out the opposite window, he tried to ignore the warmth creeping into his veins again. It was becoming clearer by the hour that Archie wasn't purging Lucy from his system; he was losing his heart and soul to her.

* * *

The Summit was a giant, glimmering, open-air shopping center that was crawling with people. The cab dropped Lucy and Gabe off at the taxi stand. He quickly paid and waded through the crush of bodies toward a boutique. Lucy felt her stomach begin to churn. "This place looks fancy…" Archie ignored Lucy and pushed open the door to the shop.

A small bell chimed, alerting the staff that customers had arrived. A moment later, a tall, slim woman dressed like she just stepped off a plane from Paris had floated over to greet them. "*Bonjour*," Her voice was thick with a French accent that Lucy instinctively knew was the real deal. This woman exuded class from every pore. "What can I assist you with today?"

"My wife needs a whole new wardrobe." Archie tugged Monster's credit card out of his wallet and handed it to her. "Whatever she needs, we'll take it."

Lucy had to bite back a chuckle as the woman's face lit up. She was going to make a lot of money off them today. The associate grabbed the tape measure that was draped across her shoulders and quickly sized Lucy up. Once she'd been measured from every angle, the saleswoman rushed off and Lucy shook her head. "Monster is really going to regret prospecting me, huh?"

"Oh, I think he already does," Archie smirked. Lucy frowned at him. "Can you at least try and enjoy this? You've been wearing Danny's hand me downs for years." He peered at her. "You used to love wearing dresses, especially in the summer."

Lucy pushed down the feelings that threatened to rise to the surface again. "My *mother* loved those pretty dresses, skirts, heels, and accessories. But me? I'm just as happy in a pair of jeans and a t-shirt." The sales associate was lining the dressing room with things for her to try. "Oh that reminds me…"Lucy bent down, undoing the ankle strap holding her handgun; she tugged her butterfly knife from her bra, and unclipped the can of mace from her belt loop before pushing them into his hands, "Hold these."

Staring at her incredulously, Archie frowned. "I can protect you, Lucy."

"Yeah, but what if I needed to protect you?" Lucy countered, leaving no room for argument. She headed to the dressing room. There were articles of clothing everywhere: fancy, lacy undergarments, silky slips, smart skirts, tasteful blouses, and—as promised—*dresses*. Lucy cursed bitterly at the emotion that clogged her throat at the sight of this. Her mother would've loved this place...and she could only imagine the joy on Louisa's face as they tried everything on together. Damn it, Lucy internally chastised herself. Why the fuck was she so weepy today?

Archie plopped down on a couch while Lucy tried things on. He could hear the rustling of clothes and her mumbled swearing. It made him smile. "How are things going in there, princess?"

Lucy rolled her eyes at Gabe's mocking pet name. She tried on a skirt with a flowing black blouse that managed to flatter and accentuate her curves at the same time. She added it to the 'buy' pile along with several new bras and matching panties. Next came the dresses. To the sales associate's credit, she hadn't picked out anything too wild. Lucy's favorite was a frock that fell just past her knee. The black silk felt buttery soft against her skin. Only the bodice was different, an overlay of delicately stitched lace covered her breasts, which showed the barest hint of cleavage peeking below the neckline. When Lucy put it on, she *did* feel like a princess. She smoothed her hands over her belly to calm the butterflies that erupted there. "How do I look?"

Archie's eyes widened as Lucy stepped out of the changing room. He stood instantly, his lips parted slightly. He almost couldn't believe his eyes. "Whoa…"

A blush crept over her cheeks, "That bad, huh?" Gazing at the tag, Lucy's mouth went dry. "Shit, this dress costs eight hundred dollars!"

"I don't care," Archie breathed. "You're getting it. As a matter of fact, you're getting all of it." Poking his head around the corner, he called the associate over. "Just wrap it up, we'll take it. Can she wear the dress out of here?"

"*Oui, monsieur,*" The woman cooed enthusiastically and hurried to package up their purchases. Gabe directed the boutique to have the rest of the items sent over to the hotel. Lucy allowed the sales associate to cut the tag off the dress and slipped into a pair of black kitten heels that fit her feet like a glove.

Lucy left the shop feeling much like Cinderella—the kitchen maid who tarted up for the big ball. Heads swiveled to stare at her as she and Gabe made their way back to the taxi stand. Once again, his large hand was pressed against the small of her back and his posture was protective. Lucy didn't fight the smile that tugged at the corners of her mouth. When they got into the cab, she snuggled against Gabe's side. The Aces High awaited and they had a job to do but she might as well enjoy these moments while they lasted.

Chapter Seven

Aces High was once the most vibrant casino on North Virginia Street. The building used to shimmer; the metal frame had once been dazzling. Now, the whole place looked brassy in the sun. The heavy glass doors that had welcomed patrons were cracked and clouded with age. An ancient carpet lined the floors, threadbare and torn in places. The color was perfectly royal red, back in the day, but had dulled to the color of mud.

Lucy crinkled her nose at the mustiness that seemed to fill every inch of the place, mingling with the scent of stale cigarettes and liquor. Straight ahead there was a rotunda with stone benches and a fountain with a cracked cherub drooling water into a dark pool. High above their heads the ceiling was pieced together with boards and plastic sheeting. It was lucky there was no rain today or water would be leaking all over the place. Pip certainly wasn't exaggerating when he said the place had gone to shit.

The main floor had a half a dozen card games in play. People in various states of dishevelment were hunched over the ancient tables, gambling for their souls. It was utterly and completely depressing. There was a long bar situated along the back wall and Archie felt like he needed a stiff one to calm his nerves. "You want a drink?"

"It's a bit too early for me, I'll pass." Plus, Lucy didn't really want to drink out of the glasses in this place; everything seemed to be covered in a thin layer of grease. The casino was laid out so that each card table had relative privacy. The one in the furthest corner was completely devoid of players; the dealer was in her sixties and plainly dressed in a pair of khaki slacks and a white blouse. She looked up, steely grey eyes boring into Lucy's onyx ones. Lucy's first instinct was to look away and join Gabe at the bar...but they were here to get information. What better way was there than talking to the locals? "I'm going to play some blackjack and see what I can find out."

Lucy fished twenty dollars out of his pocket. Archie followed her over to the table and smiled at the woman dealing cards. He watched Lucy slip the twenty onto the table and remained quiet until he realized the dealer was watching him hawkishly. "Sir, if you aren't playing, you must leave the table. House rules...we've had problems with card counters."

"Of course." Archie didn't love the idea of leaving Lucy alone but he would be nearby if she needed him. Besides, the Black Jacks had no reason to believe a young married couple would be infiltrating their casino. For good measure, Archie bent and kissed Lucy chastely on the lips, "I'm going to take a lap, sweetheart. Call if you need something." Archie kept his eyes trained on Lucy as he headed toward the bar. If anyone knew something about this place and was willing to take a bribe, Archie was betting on it being the bartender.

"Sure thing, *honey*..." Lucy found the exchange to be slightly awkward. Bedding Gabriel was one thing, playing the doting wife was quite another. Sighing softly, Lucy blushed and faced the dealer again. "How much to buy in?"

"Fifty. But the first one's on me," The dealer replied cordially. "Consider it a token of my congratulations. You are newly married, are you not?" Grey eyes slid over to where Archie was standing and she nodded appreciatively. "Young love is so very special..." There was a pause as the woman's hands rapidly shuffled the deck. "I get the sense that you married in quite a hurry..."

Lucy was immediately at ease with the woman before her. It had been so long since she'd had another woman to discuss things with. Lucy couldn't help herself. "I suppose you could say that. Gabe and I have known each other our whole lives but our wedding happened very suddenly." Lucy noticed the

83

woman's eyes dip to her waist and she laughed. "I'm not pregnant."

A knowing smile slid over the woman's features. "You are worried his feelings are not genuine?" Clucking her tongue, she dealt the cards and set the deck back on its mark. "Have no fear, dear heart. A man does not look at a woman like that if there is no love in his heart." The dealer smiled, her hands poised over the queen of hearts and six of clubs sitting in front of Lucy. The dealer had a hard nineteen; it would be very difficult to beat. "You need to decide if it is worth the risk..."

Lucy glanced over at Gabe. He was sipping a beer and chuckling with the bartender. The dealer was right; she had to decide if falling for Gabe was worth it or not. Things between them had been strained for some time...but at the end of the day, he was one risk she would always take. "Hit me." The dealer flipped a card from the top of the deck, dropping a four of clubs onto the pile. "Twenty..."

"I'll stay," Lucy grinned broadly.

"Wise choice," The dealer pushed several chips over to Lucy. "It's very important to listen to your gut when it comes to cards...and to men."

Picking up the chips, Lucy slipped them into her purse. "Thanks. I'm going to quit while I'm ahead and make sure my husband isn't getting into any trouble."

The woman bent her head in acknowledgement. "I'm Sofía Salma. I usually work in the back end, where the high rollers play. If you ever want to join us, mention my name to one of the dealers." Flashing Lucy a sly smile, she packed up her deck, "Something tells me you can keep up." Without another word, Sofía slipped behind a thick velvet curtain and disappeared from view.

Archie felt Lucy's hand slide over his back as she leaned next to him at the bar. He smiled gently and turned to face her. "How'd it go?" He hoped she had something because he was getting nowhere with the tightlipped bartender.

"Doubled my money," Lucy beamed. "And the dealer I met said I'd be welcome to play with the high rollers."

The bartender gazed up from the streaky glass he was trying to wipe out. "You're lucky Sofía took a shining to you. She doesn't usually take to strangers so easily...I probably shouldn't be telling you this but there's a big blackjack tournament tomorrow. Booze and food are free for players and their guests. You folks should stop by."

Lucy could already tell this was exactly what they needed to get a better look at how things ran here. Unfortunately, it was going to be a very expensive buy in. "How much to play?"

The bartender grinned at her knowingly. "Twenty…"

"Twenty dollars?" Archie scoffed, "That's nothing!"

"Twenty *thousand*, Gabriel," Lucy chuckled at his naïveté. "That's a serious chunk of change."

"And the payout would be many times that if you win," The bartender shrugged. "Up to you, sweetheart. Blackjack ain't a game for the faint of heart."

"We'll think about it." Lucy was ready to get out of here and tear Gabriel out of that suit. "I've had enough gambling for today. Let's go home." She slipped her winnings to the bartender with a gracious smile. In this business, it paid to have friends.

Archie remained quiet during the cab ride but Lucy was thinking so loudly he swore his head was going to explode. He waited until they were back at the hotel but once they were alone, he could stand it no longer. "How the hell are we going to come up with twenty thousand dollars, Lucy? And even if we could, we don't know what these people are up to!"

Lucy sighed heavily, "They have no idea who we are, Gabe! They just want make to money off unsuspecting idiots. This would be the perfect way to get in there without anyone realizing it. If we play our cards right, we can get an idea how the Black Jacks operate. It would be the best of all worlds." She licked her lips. "You remember what Pip said? The Black Jacks accept all sorts of bets. We don't need to have cash!"

"What exactly are you planning on leveraging?" Archie frowned.

Lucy paced the length of the room before she perched on the arm of the sofa. "Well, I have my bike…"

"You fucking love that bike, Lucy!" Normally, Lucy would never have been able to afford a Harley like the one she had. Danny's bike had been purchased for him as a rite of passage when he turned eighteen and became a prospect—it was expected. Lucy would not have been given the same gift, of course, but when Lucy's parents passed away, she received small sum from their estate. There was also an inheritance from Lucy's grandmother that she hadn't even known about until the lawyer showed her the bonds. It wasn't a fortune but Lucy was able to purchase a cherry red Harley Davidson, pay off her parents' funeral costs, and put aside a little bit for a rainy day. Since then, that bike was everything to her.

"I don't plan on losing it!" Lucy countered. "I'll bet smart and cut myself off if I start losing. It's the best option I have. If the Black Jacks are willing to trade for exotic pets and jewels, I'm sure they'd take a bet on my bike." Moving toward him again, she grasped the lapels of his suit. "You agreed this is our best shot!"

Archie had no idea how much he'd come to regret this decision later. When Lucy hands pressed against his chest, he sighed and rested his chin atop her head. It did seem like this was their best option despite the fact that Lucy would be the one doing all the legwork. "I don't like it...but you're right. We'll try it your way. "

"Good," Lucy grinned. She tilted her head back to gaze up at Archie. There was a spark of mischief in his eye that instantly lit her aflame. Before he had a chance to change his mind, she brushed her lips against his. "I've wanted you out of that suit since the minute I saw you in it," She whispered. "You should dress fancy more often."

"I could say the same thing about that dress," Archie murmured. There was no hesitation as he moved behind her, easing the dress's zipper down agonizingly slowly. He kissed every each of flesh he uncovered until he reached the small of her back. Archie wrapped his hands around Lucy's waist, tracing the curves there. The dress slipped off and pooled at her feet. Lucy's backside slid wickedly against the turgid length of him as she bent to pick the dress up. When she turned he could tell by her expression that she had done it on purpose to entice him. Archie growled low in his throat, "You little minx..."

A wry smile tugged at the corner of Lucy's lips as she turned to face him. One by one she undid the buttons on his shirt. She followed his example and she kissed down the taut muscles of his abdomen. Already Gabe's gut was clenching in anticipation, eager to take control, but Lucy wasn't going to let him. Not yet. "I get to be in charge this time," She whispered. Lucy could feel him twitching him against the zipper of his dress pants. Pure, unadulterated need was etched across his features.

Archie's breath came in harsh bursts as Lucy explored every inch of his body as if it were the first time. She tugged at the buckle of his belt so slowly; he wanted to bark at her to hurry up but her soft ministrations kept him in check. Archie had been sequestering his primal urges all afternoon and right now the beast inside him was winning over the part that wanted to savor this moment.

Tugging him toward the bed, Lucy plopped down on the mattress with a grin. She peeled his dress pants of and reveled in the sight of him bare before her. This man was all hers. Straddling him eagerly, Lucy kissed down the stubbled line of Gabe's jaw and over the thick rope of muscles at his shoulders. The twisted scar across his collarbone gave Lucy pause. Archie had scars all over his body, seen and unseen. It wrenched something open inside of her, how deeply he'd suffered at the hands of others. Lucy took inordinate time seeking out each scar, laving her tongue over the evidence of his pain in an attempt to heal him. Gabe's calloused, rough hands slid up her hips and she smiled against his lips. He begged for release and Lucy ached for it too. Finally she seated herself over him and her head tumbled back at the exquisite pleasure of taking him deep within her.

Bucking instinctively, Archie let out a harsh groan. He grasped her hips, holding her steady as she rocked against him. The angle was fantastic for both of them. It didn't take long before he was swept away by need. Archie wasn't sure why she chose tonight to explore his soul but he lost himself to her completely. Holding her tighter as he rode out the concussive force of his orgasm, he absolutely knew...the feelings he had for Lucy weren't an infatuation.

He loved her.

It wasn't just a teenage crush. The realization terrified him. Archie could never offer Lucy a real marriage, family, or a promise of forever. To do so would be setting them up for failure. Eventually, she'd realize he was a monster but it would be too late for her to run from him. The thought of hurting Lucy made Archie sick to his stomach. Carefully, he pushed her aside and sat at the edge of the bed, dragging his hands through his hair.

"What's wrong?" Lucy was still breathless. She lay on her side, staring at him as he brooded. He looked tormented and angry; two emotions she was not expecting after the sensual moment they shared. As they made love, it felt different...like their two souls had intertwined. When he didn't answer, Lucy sat up. "Gabe?" She inched closer and slipped her hands over his shoulders. She gasped in surprise when he tore away from her. "Gabriel!"

"This was a mistake." Archie couldn't bear to face her. Lucy was the most beautiful woman he'd ever seen and he had let this get very out of hand. "Once we figure this Black Jack thing out, we're going back to Errol and the first thing we're going to do it get this marriage annulled."

Lucy felt as if she'd been slapped. "Don't you mean get a divorce?" A chill crept over her and she pulled the blanket from the bed around her naked form. They'd consummated the union; it wasn't something that could just be undone. Lucy shivered. "What's gotten into you? I thought we were having fun." Her expression soured. "You can't tell me you didn't enjoy yourself."

Archie couldn't lie about that. This time with Lucy was the most pleasurable experience in his entire life. When he was with her, the darkness inside him seemed so far away...but he always knew it was there, lurking and waiting to strike. Archie shored up his defenses, putting on his most apathetic face. "We fucked, I feel better, and I don't want to do it again. We've got more important things to do..." Disgust churned in his stomach from the bitterness of his pain. "I'm going to take a shower." The more distance he put between them, the better off they'd both be.

Lucy had gone from absolute blissful euphoria to feeling like her heart had been torn in pieces. Just twenty minutes ago, he couldn't keep his eyes or hands off her. Which meant he was purposely pushing her away...she just couldn't figure out why. They were right back at square one. Lucy was furious. "You're a coward, you know that?"

Archie was almost in the bathroom when Lucy's defiant voice reached his ears. He turned to glare at her. "What the hell did you just say?"

"I *said* you're a fucking coward!" Lucy pointed an accusatory finger at him. "Don't forget I know you better than anyone else, Gabriel. I know when you're happy, I know when you're sad, and I know when you're hurting." She held the blanket tighter against her body as she confronted him. "You do not look like a man who's decided he's done fucking his wife!" Lucy paused. "We have something here. Why are you fighting it?"

"I'm done with you, Lucy. Drop it!" Archie felt his control slipping away.

"I don't take orders from you, Gabriel Stephen Archer!"

That thin shred holding him together snapped violently as he turned to face her. "Don't you fucking get it, Lucy? You can't get sucked into my shit and end up a crumbling, broken, crying woman putting your child on an airplane to get him the fuck away from me! I won't let you become a casualty of the Archer curse!"

Lucy's head spun. "Gabe, you are *not* your father!" He didn't move and judging from the expression on his face, he didn't believe her. Lucy stalked to his side. "You are *not* Erik Archer, damn it!" She cried. "I've known you my entire life. You'd never lay a hand on me!" Lucy grasped Gabe's shoulders, the blanket falling away to leave her naked and exposed to him. "How many times have I pissed you off, Gabriel? I don't think we could count them if we wanted to." She narrowed her eyes. "Did you ever *once* want to bash my face in?"

"No!" Archie cried raggedly, "Fuck no, Lucy. Never!" His response was automatic. Still, he gritted his teeth, remembering his actions with shame and regret after he learned she became a prospect. "But I beat the shit out of Monster…"

"You punched Monster *once* in the eye. It bruised. He didn't up in the hospital on life support! He went home, cursed your name to his wife, cracked open a bottle of whiskey, and moved on!" Lucy wished she could grab Gabe and shake sense into him. "If anything, your leniency is even more a testament to the fact that you're different from your father. Monster used *your* proxy vote knowing full well that you'd never have allowed me to prospect. He

93

betrayed you and walked away unscathed." She reached for him again.

Archie dodged Lucy's embrace, desperate to keep her at bay. "Don't make excuses for me. That's how it starts! That's how it was for my mother. I'm bad news, Lucy, and I won't let you get caught up in my hell." He needed to put distance between them before she broke through and he was unable to resist her. "It doesn't matter what you say. You're not going to change my mind." Archie stalked into the bathroom, slamming the door closed and locking it. His forehead rested against the wood as the battle for sanity raged on.

Lucy's throat felt tight and her blood boiled with anger. "You can't fight this forever, Gabe," She hollered at the closed door. Stomping over, she slammed her first against it, just once. Gabe was right on the other side of that door but they were hundreds of miles apart.

For her sake, he hoped that wasn't true. Archie stepped away from the bathroom door, turning shower as hot as it would go. He needed to wash her scent off him, purge the desire from his heart, and find the strength to keep her at arm's length. Stepping beneath the brutal spray, he gritted his teeth against the burning of his skin. Archie reminded himself that loneliness was a fate far preferable to hurting the woman he loved. If he stayed with Lucy, it would only end in heartbreak for both of them.

Chapter Eight

While Gabe hid in the shower, Lucy changed into a pair of jeans and t-shirt. Although she wanted to cry, scream, and curse but she felt paralyzed. What Lucy needed in this moment was comfort and stability and she knew of only one way to get it. Grabbing her cellphone, she stalked out onto the balcony and plopped down, letting her legs dangle over the railing. Dialing the familiar number for home, she closed her eyes and listened to it ring.

"*Who is it?*"

"Danny?" Lucy was so grateful to hear his voice that she nearly wept. Wrapping her arm tighter around herself, she swallowed past the lump in her throat. "How are you?"

Danny was quiet for a long moment. "Lucy, what's wrong?"

"Why do you think something is wrong?" Lucy asked, wondering how he could have possibly figured that out. Maybe he had suddenly become attuned to her feelings?

"You never call here. Something must be up," Danny replied.

"That's not true," Lucy snapped irritably. Leave it to Danny to start an argument over nothing—or maybe she was just looking for a fight tonight. "I haven't been gone this long in a while and I wanted to make sure you were alright…"

"I'm fine. And no I didn't throw any wild parties, *mom*," Danny drawled. "Come on, Luce. Cut the shit. You may think I belong riding the short bus but I can tell when you're upset. So either tell me what the fuck is wrong or I'm hanging up on you!"

Lucy snorted suddenly, ignoring the prick of tears in her eyes. "Fine, you're right…I've been fighting with Gabe."

Danny's raspy laugh echoed through the receiver. "What else is new?" Lucy could hear the mirth in his voice. "What'd you do this time?"

Sitting up straighter, Lucy huffed indignantly, "Why'd you assume *I* did something?"

"You're *always* the instigator."

"Oh I see, this is a bro code thing. Whatever happened to family loyalty?" Lucy sighed and stared out over the twisting, whirling lights of the city. A heavy silence hung between them before Lucy spoke again. "Did you two ever talk about his father?"

Danny scoffed, "No! Nobody wants to talk about that shit. You were a baby when Archie came to live with us. You didn't see the state he was in when he first got off that plane." He let out a rumbling sigh. "I remember we went to the doctor the next day.

Archie's arm had been repeatedly broken and never set properly. They had to break it *again* and he wore a cast for almost a year…"

Lucy's stomach ached with sadness. "What else do you remember?"

"I *remember* that Archie doesn't fucking talk about this stuff and wouldn't appreciate you sticking your big fat nose into things," Danny chastised. "Leave it the hell alone, Luce! He's got enough shit to worry about without you trying to talk about feelings or whatever the hell you girls try to do to us."

"I do not have a big fat nose!" Just like that, she was back to bickering with Danny like they were children and order was restored to her world. "I hope you're staying out of trouble, Danny. Seriously, if I come back to that house and it's a sty, I'm going to kick your ass six ways from Sunday." A long silence told her that it was already wrecked in there. "Call up one the prospects and get him to clean it. Hunter or Kyle…not Mort. He's sweet but I don't think the boy can find his ass with both hands and a flashlight."

Danny chuckled appreciatively. "Good idea." He sobered. "Do me a favor and try to have fun, please? Leave Archie alone. Not everything has to be so damn serious."

That was rich coming from Danny, who took absolutely *nothing* seriously. "Alright. I love you, big brother."

"Love you too, little sis. Remember what I said." Danny disconnected the call, leaving Lucy's cell phone beeping on her end. Punching the off button, she headed back the bedroom and glanced around. Gabe was *still* showering in an attempt to avoid confrontation. Lucy sighed and flicked on the television. Although she wasn't really hungry, she ordered them some dinner before hunkering down to get lost in some sappy romantic comedy. Usually it wasn't her type of film but she needed a distraction from the hurt that welled up inside her. Lucy wanted to believe happily ever after could really happen, even if it was only for an hour.

Gabe stepped out of the bathroom just as the room service cart was being wheeled in. Lucy tipped the man handsomely and grabbed the macaroni and cheese she'd ordered. It was the ultimate comfort food—exactly what she needed right now. Lucy decided against pettiness and broke the silence between them, "I got you a burger," She announced.

Archie finished drying his hair and tossed the towel onto the rack. "Thanks." He sat down and picked at the meal in front of him. Although it was perfectly fine, he really didn't feel like eating. Eventually he gave up and set it aside. He realized Lucy was doing the same exact thing; they were just going through the motions to avoid awkwardness. Gabe poured two glasses of booze from the mini bar. Holding one of the cups out to Lucy, he said nothing as she refused the drink. With a shrug, he simply poured her scotch into his glass. "I'm going to sleep on the sofa tonight..."

Lucy caught her bottom lip between her teeth to steel herself against the onslaught of emotion. "Fine." Danny was right. Rome wasn't built in a day and she wasn't going to be able to get through to Gabriel in one either. Lucy went searching through the armoire until she came up with some extra sheets and a blanket. "Here." If she just kept it cordial, treating him as if they were casual acquaintances, everything would be okay.

Archie's eyes swept over her. He never thought in a million years that her reserved, cold demeanor would be worse than her anger. He felt like he was the lowest scum on the earth. Despite the confusion it would cause, he wanted nothing more than to wrap her up in his arms and kiss it better...but that would defeat the purpose of everything he was trying to do. It was too early for bed but he settled on the couch nonetheless. Lucy flicked through the channels until she found some stupid romantic comedy. Archie marveled at the stupidity of a man who thought he could build a relationship on lies. Those thoughts haunted him as he drifted into a fitful sleep.

Sometime around midnight, Lucy shut off the TV. Gabe was snoring lightly on the couch, one leg

99

thrown over the back of it and his arm hanging off and draping on the floor. She grabbed the blanket and pulled it over him. Sighing softly, she leaned down and dropped a gentle kiss on his forehead before shutting out the light. Exhaustion overtook her as she slid into the big, empty bed and closed her eyes. Today had been a disaster but things would be clearer in the morning...they had to be.

Chapter Nine

When Lucy awoke the next morning, she was alone. She wandered aimlessly around the suite until she noticed a pad of paper sitting on the table. Gabe had penned a quick note about going to pick up breakfast. Lucy took the opportunity to look through the purchases they'd made yesterday. A black pencil skirt and simple white blouse were neatly pressed and hanging in the closet. Additionally, there was a pair of grey dress pants and a sateen top with several tastefully sexy cutouts. In the far corner of the closet hung a dress that would be perfect for tonight's blackjack game. The crimson gown was floor length and sparkled with sequins. After a quick shower, she decided to try it on and was pleasantly surprised by how sensual yet modest the piece really was. It was truly perfect.

Archie pushed open the door to the suite to find Lucy modeling a dress he could only assume was intended to give him a heart attack. She looked like a siren, fresh and dewy from her shower, luring him to his death. Archie narrowly avoided dumping the coffee as he tripped over his own two feet. "Shit!" He carefully placed everything on the table before he could spill it everywhere.

Lucy whirled around, unaware that he'd returned. "Hey…" She chewed her bottom lip. "I was just picking out an outfit for tonight. What do you think?"

"You look amazing." Archie bit back a curse at how enamored he sounded right now. He cleared his throat several times to try and get rid of the admiration in his voice. "I got you the same coffee as yesterday, I hope that's okay."

"That was very thoughtful of you, thanks." To preserve the gown for tonight's affairs, she changed into a pair of holey jeans and a tank top. It wouldn't do to risk such a fancy dress becoming wrinkled or stained. She grabbed the coffee from the tray and sighed at the delicious infusion of caffeine. "Mmm, that's good." He'd also gotten egg sandwiches and she grabbed the one with an L written on it. Her eyes widened when she took a bite. "You remembered I like jalapeños in my eggs?"

Gabe plopped down on the couch and took a long swig of his own coffee. "Of course I remember. I grew up with you, Luce. I know everything there is to know about you and your crazy, weird food preferences."

"Liking your eggs spicy is not weird!" Lucy groused. "You hate peanut butter and jelly. *That* is insane."

101

"I don't *hate* it," Archie replied curtly. "I just don't see what all the hype is about. It's peanut butter and jelly and bread, *not* the second coming of the messiah." He raised his palms in mock surrender, "I know you love your PB&J but I'll take a turkey club any day." For a moment, it almost felt like the old days when they could sit and talk all day. It was a simpler time then, long before he realized he was in love with Lucy.

"Agree to disagree," Lucy chuckled softly and finished off the rest of her sandwich. Now that she had her coffee, she was fully conscious and ready to tackle whatever today threw at her. "So what about these prospects you had lined up? Do we have meetings today?"

"Not we. *Me*." Archie narrowed his eyes, "No arguments! I can't have a prospect hanging around for this. It doesn't matter if you're male or female or a fucking ghost, it's not the way these things are done. Only members can meet with prospects. I need to make sure these guys are solid if we're going to start up a charter in Reno."

Lucy knew the rules of the MC but this town was dangerous, uncharted territory. There were potential enemies everywhere and she'd be damned if she let Gabe get hurt. "What if something goes south?"

Archie's frown deepened. "If something goes south then I want you as far away as possible, Lucy. This isn't your fight."

"The hell it isn't! The Black Jacks gunned my parents down in the street. This is personal! I want to see the them wiped off the Earth just as badly as the rest of you." Lucy pressed. "I don't need to be at your side while you talk to these guys but Gabriel, I'm begging you...don't go off half cocked just because you're trying to push me away." Lucy felt her chest begin to ache with sadness again. "Look, I understand why you don't want to try. I'm resigned to the fact that you aren't going to give us a chance..."

"Lucy—"

She folded her arms over her chest. "I'm not trying to restart the fight. I'm just saying, I can compartmentalize my feelings too. It's not that hard. I'll just imagine you're an overbearing, pig-headed dick." Her onyx eyes narrowed again. "Actually, I think it's going to be easier than I ever imagined!" Lucy was not backing down. "I will not get in your way. I will not listen in. But I just can't let you go walking in there knowing something could happen to you when I could have stopped it."

Once again, Archie found himself pinching the bridge of his nose in a vain attempt to stop a tension headache before it began. Lucy wasn't wrong; this was unfamiliar territory and there was a strong possibility it could become hostile. So far they'd avoided detection but the Black Jacks weren't stupid. Still, he hated the idea of putting Lucy anywhere near a dangerous situation. If anything happened to her, he would never recover. Then again, if he didn't give her the go ahead, she would still find a way to be there and that could cause even more trouble down the line. Archie took a deep breath and capitulated. *"Fine.* You can come but you stay out of sight and you don't interfere unless I ask for your help. Am I understood?"

"Yeah, boss, coming in loud and clear." Lucy strapped her gun to her ankle, placed the butterfly knife back into its spot at her ribcage, and clipped the mace to her belt loop.

Tamping down on the urge to roll his eyes, Gabe ushered her out of the suite. They headed to the same dingy lounge where they'd interviewed Pip yesterday. Lucy sat at the bar sipping water while Gabe met with several young men who were eager to become part of the Devil's Own. The comforting hum of motorcycle engines coming and going outside was a welcome change from the squeaking of taxi breaks and thunderous boom of busses dropping off passengers.

It was just after noon when a group of men in suits filed into the bar to enjoy a drink. Lucy didn't think anything of it until one of them moved beside her. "This seat taken?" He was passably handsome with wispy, white blonde hair, cut close to his head. Lucy was guessing he was probably ex-military. His dark brown eyes were jolly and kind. Even with the lifts on his dress shoes, he was several inches shorter than she. Since he posed no threat, Lucy shrugged.

The man slipped into the seat beside her and signaled for the bartender. "I'll have what she's having."

"You're going to be disappointed, buddy." Lucy chuckled to herself. "I've got water."

"Seven years sober." He grinned and extended his hand to her, "Steve Ellis...esquire."

"Well Steve Ellis, esquire, that's probably a good choice then." Lucy made sure there was no way he could miss the wedding rings on her hand when treating him to an extra-firm handshake. "Lucy Archer..." Even though Lucy wasn't looking at him, she could feel Gabe's eyes at her back. If he was going to play the part of jealous husband, she was going to put on a show. Lucy pasted a grin on her face and took another sip of her water. "What's a guy seven years sober doing in a dump like this?"

Steve wrapped his hand around his glass. "What's a classy chick like you doing at the nastiest bar in Reno?"

"I asked you first," Lucy replied tartly.

Steve motioned to the collection of suits ordering shots. "Last Friday of the month the whole office takes a half day. They get trashed and I make sure they get home without killing themselves or anyone else. Right now, I've got everyone's house and car keys. I'm surprised you didn't hear me jingling from all the way outside."

Lucy's soft, feminine laughter elicited a primal response from Archie. He was desperately trying to ignore the fact that she was talking to some jerk in a suit and appeared to be having a nice conversation. His jaw clenched in anger and he forgot to listen to the boy in front of him droning on about his dreams of being part of the MC.

"So this is something you do every month? What's the boss have to say about that?" Lucy smirked.

Steve winked playfully. "I don't mind. It boosts morale and promotes teamwork."

It didn't surprise Lucy that Steve was the man in charge; there was an air of authority about him. Something in the way he carried himself told her that he put his all into everything he did. "That's smart. Happy workers do better work."

"We haven't lost a case yet." Steve boasted, "Although I think our winning streak is mostly due to the fact that we put away murderers, rapists, and child abusers."

"You decided to lead with that?" Lucy snorted, "I'm guessing you're not married? Or at least not anymore…" Steve bristled slightly and Lucy knew she hit the nail on the head. "Let me give you a piece of advice?"

"Please," Steve listened raptly.

Lucy rested her hand on his shoulder. "You're kinda funny, you've got a good job, and you're smart…but you're cocky." He leaned in closer—in what she could only assume was an attempt to kiss her. Lucy put two fingers on Steve's forehead and gently pushed his head back. "*But* you come on a little strong." She frowned markedly. "For example, I'm not hitting on you." She tilted her head. "Do you see that behemoth in the corner? That's my husband."

Steve shrank away from her the second he realized his mistake. "Oh…" He cleared his throat and slipped off the stool, nervously glancing over to the booth in the back.

Lucy raised an eyebrow and glanced over at Gabe again. The vein in the middle of Gabe's forehead was throbbing and his hand was clenched tight around his glass; but he hadn't lost control just yet. "If you keep your hands to yourself from now on, you should be fine." She motioned for Steve to sit down again. "As I was saying, you misread signals and get in trouble. I notice you don't have any women working with your little group…narrowly dodged a few sexual harassment suits?" He was silent and Lucy smirked. "That's what I thought."

"What should I do about it?"

"Well for one thing, you don't just lean in and kiss a girl. Ask her out on a date first. If she wants to go to dinner with you, chances are she might entertain the idea of kissing you." Lucy explained. "Play it cool. Talk about books or the weather or music before you go delving into the deeper stuff. She doesn't need to know you're seven years sober before she knows what kind of food you like." Lucy smirked.

For a moment, Steve sat with that thought. "Thank you." Reaching into his pocket, he pulled out a card and slid it over to her. "If you ever need a lawyer, call me up. Lucy Archer, it has been a pleasure." He grasped her hand and dropped an overly dramatic kiss to her knuckles.

"Alright, that's enough," Lucy laughed quietly as Steve walked away. The man was harmless; he reminded her so much of Anita it was almost uncanny. When she turned back to her drink, Lucy found herself face to face with a very annoyed Gabe. "Is there a problem, sweetheart?"

"What the hell was that?" Archie snapped and picked the business card up off the bar. "Flirting with lawyers?" Jealousy stole over him and burned hot in his gut. "We're supposed to be newlyweds."

Lucy stood toe to toe with her very jealous husband. "I wasn't flirting, Gabriel. He was coming onto me and I very nicely explained that he didn't have a shot in hell." She lowered her voice. "Besides, what do you care? At least when you divorce me, I'll have a couple dates lined up."

Archie gritted his teeth angrily. "Oh, so you're going to take my ring off your finger and immediately jump into the next guy's bed? You're just going to pretend none of this ever happened?" The rage that burned in his chest was intensely uncomfortable.

"Move on from *what*, Gabriel?" Lucy glowered. "You made yourself very clear last night. You are not interested in having any kind of relationship with me, sexual or otherwise. So yeah, I'm going to do my best to pretend that this was all a very erotic bad dream and move on like you told me to!"

"Damn it, Lucy!"

She poked her finger into Gabe's chest. "You don't get to have this both ways! You can't expect me to turn my feelings on and off like a faucet. If you want to be with me, it's all or nothing. You either give in to what we both clearly know is between us or you butt out and let me live my life."

Archie knew he wasn't playing fair. He had no right to be jealous or possessive but damn it, he couldn't help himself. Averting his gaze, he mumbled a hasty, "I'm sorry."

"What was that? An actual *apology* from Gabriel Archer?" Lucy feigned shock and dismay. "Hold on, I need to put this down on my calendar. This is one for the history books!"

"You're a fucking riot," Archie snarked sarcastically.

Flashing him a grin, Lucy rested her hand on the bar. "Did you have any luck with the prospects?" She'd formed her own opinions about them as they came in but—in deference to the MC's rules—she kept her mouth shut.

"Mickey and Ralph are my top choices. They'll be great additions to the club." Archie could sense her approval and it made him smile. He was glad she agreed, even if she didn't really have a say. "It's going to be a late one tonight. What do you say we head back to the room, pick a movie, and relax?"

"You must've read my mind," Lucy sighed. There hadn't been much sleeping the first three days in Reno and the last two nights she'd only gotten a couple hours here or there. A nap sounded heavenly right now.

Lucy and Gabe walked back to the hotel in silence. When they got back to the room, each of them went their separate ways and things were peaceful. *Maybe the worst of it is over*, Lucy thought. Or maybe it was yet to come.

Chapter Ten

The afternoon passed in the blink of an eye. Lucy was hogging the bathroom as she primped for a night out on the town. Archie reluctantly started dressing but his inexperience with formalwear was causing problems. "Can you help me? My suit is all wrinkled." He owned jeans, t-shirts, and a couple flannel button downs—nothing that ever needed to get ironed. He was afraid he was going to end up ruining his only nice outfit. "Please?"

"Yeah, sure." Lucy set the iron up to heat while she fought her curly hair. Shaking out the tight curls, she spritzed them with a bit of water before sweeping up half of her hair with a clip they'd purchased at the boutique. It served to keep the unruliness under control—at least for the moment. Lucy applied just a dab of makeup, enough to accentuate the blush of her cheeks and the plumpness of her lips. Shimmying into the dress again, she turned her back to Gabe. "Can you zip me, please?"

Archie's breath caught in his throat at the sight of her. Lucy was the most elegant woman he'd ever seen. "Sure," he said gruffly and worked the zipper up. Despite his best efforts, his fingertips lingered on the creamy skin of her shoulders. One second longer and he'd have been swept away by desire. Thankfully, Lucy pulled away before he succumbed.

Ignoring the flush of her cheeks, Lucy faked a smile. "Thanks." Her traitorous body was ached for his touch, but now wasn't the time. They were due at Aces High in an hour. Circumventing Gabe, she ironed out the wrinkles in the suit with ease and handed them over to him. "That should do it."

Slipping them on over his lean hips, Gabe straightened his tie. He took a moment to peer at their reflections in the mirror. There was no denying they were an extremely handsome couple. Gabe's hand snaked out and gently grasped her wrist. "You can still back out, you know. You don't have to do this."

"Yes, I do," Lucy smiled sadly. "For the club, for my family...for *us.* The sooner we get this out of the way, the sooner we go home and end this charade." She smoothed the front of her dress. "Besides, it's just a couple hands of blackjack. What's the worst that could happen?"

Archie didn't respond. There were millions of things that could go wrong...but he simply shrugged and ushered her out of the room. A limousine was waiting for them when they got out onto the street. "Did you do this?" Lucy faced Gabe, her expression incredulous. Her surprise only grew when the chauffeur informed her that Aces High provided transportation for her tonight, free of charge. It was a service they extended to high rollers and friends of the casino. As Lucy slipped into the buttery leather seats, she raised an eyebrow at the expensive champagne that had been opened just for them.

Archie eagerly reached for a glass and sniffed it once before taking a sip. "It's actually really good. You want some?"

Lucy shook her head and leaned back in her seat. "This is all a tactic to get me to loosen up. Free booze and food will make me drunk and tired, then I won't worry as much about placing a risky bet. I need to keep my wits about me." Now more than ever.

"More for me," Archie grinned. He sat several inches away from Lucy but every time the massive limo turned a corner, they ended up sliding together. Archie ached to kiss her pouty lips and explore the flesh that the dress revealed...instead he dug his nails into his palm and stared out the window.

Lucy shifted uncomfortably in the silence that lingered between them. It was a blessed relief when they pulled up in front of the casino and were no longer trapped at each other's side. Dozens of vehicles idled in front of the aging sidewalk, which had been covered over by red carpet.

Aces High was in rare form tonight. Garlands of blinking, twirling lights twinkled around the doors. There were butlers in tuxedos who opened doors and waiters were standing by to take drink orders. Multiple people offered her food and drinks as they navigate the place. Lucy waved them off and headed toward the main event. Music from a live jazz band filled every corner of the room. Just another way the casino was trying to distract her into losing money. She could hardly think it was so loud!

Archie's hand instinctively rested on the curve of Lucy's spine as they followed the crowd toward the main stage. He caught sight of Sofía standing by the wall, speaking quietly but frantically to a woman dressed in black. They seemed to be agreeing about something but with all the people around, he couldn't make out a word. When the woman turned around, Archie was almost positive he saw her wearing a Black Jack cut... No, that couldn't be right. He shrugged it off.

Seconds later, the musicians quieted and the soft squealing of a microphone echoed through the room. "Hello and welcome to Aces High Casino and Lounge. You are our most treasured friends, guests, and benefactors—" The speaker paused for appreciative laughter and slipped onto the main stage area. Sofía smiled ear to ear as she held the microphone close to her painted ruby lips. "On behalf of all of our staff, we would like to wish you the very best of luck in our annual blackjack tournament. The buy in stands at twenty thousand dollars. Ladies and gentleman, if you win tonight you could walk away with over a million dollars!" A gasp tore through the crowd, followed by more hushed whispers.

Archie gazed over at Lucy and immediately knew she was daunted. Reaching out, he slipped his hand into hers and was rewarded with a bright smile that practically melted his heart. He smiled back at her lovingly.

"Each player will receive a number at buy-in. Play as many hands as you wish until you make it big or go home broke. Staff will be on hand to get you anything you want and the buffet station is open now. Players may join us in the Regent Room. Happy gambling!" Once Sofía set the microphone down, the band started up again and people went back to talking and laughing.

"This is it…" Archie turned to face Lucy once more. "Are you ready?"

Lucy nodded, following the signage toward the Regent Room. She immediately noticed several people wearing cuts emblazoned with the Black Jacks' logo. Lucy would've recognized it anywhere; their insignia was a jack of hearts and the ace of hearts held by a skeletal hand that dripped with blood. Both she and Archie were on high alert. They were in enemy territory…one wrong move and they'd both be killed.

When finally Lucy and Gabe approached the buy-in line, Lucy slipped a picture of her Harley Davidson out of her purse. The woman at the front of the table glanced down at it and tilted her head to Lucy but the moment Gabe moved to follow, she stopped him. "Players only beyond this point."

Gritting his teeth, Archie opened his mouth to argue but Lucy cut him off swiftly, "Don't worry, sweetheart. I won't lose all my money." She stood on tiptoe, kissing him sweetly. For just a moment, his lips lingered. Lucy knew the kiss was for show but this seemed as good an excuse as any to savor it.

Archie reluctantly disentangled himself from her arms and took a step back. "I'll be right outside."

"Go enjoy the buffet and the open bar. If I need something I will come find you." Lucy narrowed her eyes. "Have fun!" It was obvious from his expression that he hated this with a fiery passion, but he was already getting the evil eye from the bitch guarding the door. Once Gabe had left, Lucy found herself face to face with Sofía again. "This is quite the setup you've got here," she smiled broadly.

Sofía's mouth was twisted into a Cheshire cat smile. "I am so happy that you have accepted my invitation, *mija*. Come, come, I've reserved you a place." Ushering Lucy over to a quiet table, set away from the rest of the players, Sofía opened up a brand new deck of cards.

Lucy thought nothing of Sofía's offer until she found herself surrounded by three women, all wearing Black Jacks cuts. Lucy glanced around, a sense of dread rising in her chest. Sofía seemed unperturbed as she shuffled the cards, her piercing grey eyes accentuated by the massive opal pendant hanging from her neck. Sofía's movements slowed as she cut the deck and dealt the cards. Right off the bat, Lucy was in the lead. "Dealer busts. You win."

A cold sweat broke out over Lucy's back as Sofía slid a pile of chips toward Lucy. Something was very wrong here. Two of the women sitting around her were near Lucy's age and fairly nondescript. The other one was a slim, gaunt-looking brunette who wore thick corrective glasses; the tag on her chest read 'Millie'. She was glaring at Lucy menacingly as Sofía dealt a second hand.

"Do not be afraid, *querida*," Sofía crooned. "They will not hurt you. You are a kindred spirit. I could tell from the very the moment you drove through the gates of my city." Sofía rested palms on the table as she met Lucy's gaze. "Your husband, however…he is my enemy."

Ice filled Lucy's veins, mixing with a boiling hot vat of anger. "What do you want?" She snarled. "My bike? Take it!" Her heart was starting to pound as she watched the wolves begin to circle her.

Millie's hand was immediately wrapped around her gun but Sofía glared at her until she backed down. Sofía shook her head to halt the woman's movement. "I don't wish to take *anything* from you, Lucy." When she leaned back, the neckline of her shirt tugged to reveal the Black Jacks insignia tattooed across her chest. "In fact, I am here to offer you the deal of a lifetime." When she snapped her fingers, a girl no older than seventeen trotted out with a heavy leather cut with Lucy's name emblazoned on it. "I took the liberty of having this made up for you…"

"I don't know what the fuck is going on here but I'm no Black Jack. I'm a Devil!" Lucy snapped. "But you already knew that, didn't you?"

Sofía remained ice cold. "I am aware of everything that goes on in my city." She smiled coldly. "That is where your club of misfits and losers went wrong. They believe they are invincible. They take no precautions to protect themselves, which makes them sitting ducks."

"At least the Devils don't run around killing innocent people," Lucy seethed, her voice rising in anger. "If you're so fucking smart then you already know my parents were murdered by the Black Jacks! I would never in a million years consider joining you."

"That was the old Black Jacks," Sofía replied. "I am sorry for the loss you suffered but I can assure you, things are very different now. The old dogs have been purged from the club. It is a brand new day for us. We are looking for smart riders. Those who will bring intellect and strength of character to the club. It is no wonder the majority of our positions are held by women. You will be quite impressed with our organization, I'm sure." She folded her hands.

"Go on, try on your new cut. I think it will look perfect!"

Lucy couldn't believe what was happening. "No! I won't betray my family, my friends, and my club for this bullshit!" She snapped. "I don't know what kind of harem your boss thinks he's running but I won't be a part of it!"

Sofía raised an eyebrow. "He?" A mirthful chuckle tumbled from her lips. "*Querida*, you have been misled." She smirked. "It's an easy mistake. People assume the leader of the largest and most powerful MC in Nevada would be run by someone much like your husband." Her gaze hardened. "*I* am Sofía Salma, *Presidente* of the Black Jacks."

If Lucy had been standing, she was sure she'd have tumbled over in shock. "You...*you're* Sal?" Suddenly things started falling into place. Pip kept calling Sal a 'bitch'; he wasn't just pushed out because of his infirmity but because he was a man in a woman's club. Rubbing her temples, she let out a shaky breath, "This doesn't change anything. I'm all for *girl power* but I'm loyal to my blood."

"I had feared you would say that..." Sofía's smile remained plastered on her face. "What do you say we make it interesting? We play for it."

"I said *no*," Lucy growled.

"Don't you want to hear the wager, *mija*?" Without waiting for Lucy's answer, Sofía forged ahead. "You play this hand or I kill your husband."

The monitors watching the main floor were turned so Lucy could see them. Gabe was standing aimlessly by the bar, sipping a beer and chewing an appetizer. He was chatting with a stranger, unaware that there were two Black Jacks in the ballroom with guns trained on him. Lucy's breath hitched in her throat. "Don't you dare hurt him, you crazy bitch!"

"That is what I thought," Sofía chuckled darkly. With expert skill, she dealt new cards. The dealer's cards totaled eighteen, and Lucy's only twelve. "You win this hand and you are free to go. Lose, and you will patch to the Black Jacks. You will be one of us. Sisters in arms…" Her face remained twisted by a smile. "That seems a very fair deal. Is it not, ladies?"

The Black Jacks sitting all around Lucy were nodding and murmuring to each other. Lucy's stomach clenched in disgust. Giving in to the whims of a madwoman was not at all what she wanted to do but Lucy would be damned if she allowed anything to happen to Gabriel. She'd give up far more than her bike to protect him. "Hit me." Her voice wavered only slightly.

Time came to a screeching halt. Lucy was no longer aware of voices or music, the lights seemed to dim and concentrate over Sofía's hands, and the only thing Lucy could see was that card. Letting out a shaky breath, she watched her life crumble before her eyes as Sofía laid down the queen of hearts. *Bust*.

It was all over. She belonged to the Black Jacks now.

"Congratulations, Lucy. You're one of us now." Sofía stood and stepped behind her and slid the warm leather cut over her shoulders. Bending to Lucy's ear, Sofía whispered so only she would be able to hear. "You will learn to be happy, *querida*. One day you will look back on and realize is the best decision you have ever made."

Lucy's throat was dry and her lips chapped as she turned to face Sofía. "What *decision*? You forced my hand!" She protested.

"In time you will come to see it differently. They all do," Sofía replied cordially. "You'll have the evening to say goodbye to your husband and in the morning, a car will pick you up. Let me be clear, Lucy. If Gabriel returns to Reno again, it will not just be his wife that we take from him." The threat lingered in the air. "You may send for your bike. Buy the rest of what you need." Leaning in, Sofía gingerly kissed Lucy's cheek. "Welcome to the Black Jacks." With that, she turned and swept out of the room.

* * *

Nausea churned in Lucy's veins and her vision swam dangerously, causing her to sway on her feet.

121

Breathe, Lucy reminded herself. She hadn't been so off-kilter since the day she found out her parents had been killed. Sofia claimed the Black Jacks were different but Lucy didn't believe them. The same Black Jacks that murdered her family had now claimed her life in a very different way.

Somehow, Lucy managed to put one foot in front of the other. Ignoring the cold glances of people scattered around the room, she staggered back into the ballroom. She locked eyes on Gabe immediately and pushed her way through the crowd to get to him. "We have to go…" Her voice was thick with desperation and fear. "Now!"

Archie had never stopped worrying about Lucy. Seeing the state she was in now did nothing to allay those fears. Grasping her shoulder, he furrowed his eyebrows at the vest draped over her gown. "What the hell are you wearing?" His eyes widened in shock when he spun her around and saw the Black Jack logo emblazoned across her back. "Lucy, what the fuck is going on?"

"Not here," Lucy begged and grasped his wrist. "I need to go, I need to—" Inhaling sharply, she felt panic clawing at her chest. Lucy's knees grew weak and she would've ended up in a crumpled heap on the floor if not for Gabe's strong arms wrapping around her. The next thing she knew, he was carrying her out of the stuffy, crowded casino. Lucy threaded her arms around his neck, desperate to absorb some of his strength.

122

Fear slammed into Archie's chest. Right now, he didn't care that she was wearing the colors of another MC, their sworn enemies; he just needed to make sure she would be okay. "Should I call an ambulance? Are you sick?" She didn't feel feverish but she was certainly flushed and shaking.

"The hotel..." Lucy rasped. "Take me back to the hotel." Instead of getting into the limo, they stole the first taxi rolled up. Her icy fingers tangled in Gabe's dress shirt as they drove in silence. When they got out and she went to pay, the cab driver shook his head; Black Jack members paid nothing in this city. This time when her stomach roiled, she barely made it to the bathroom in their suite before she retched until nothing came up but bile. Once the gagging stopped, Lucy ripped off the leather cut she'd been forced to wear and threw it into a heap.

Archie paced outside the bathroom door, his heart thundered in his chest. "Lucy, I need to know you're okay!" It wasn't often he felt the cold grip of fear's hand wrapped around his heart and lungs, but Lucy was his everything. He wouldn't rest until this was resolved.

"No, I'm not okay!" Lucy's face was wet and hot with tears as she gripped the porcelain bowl of the toilet so tightly she feared it would crumble beneath her hands. Dragging herself up, she plopped down on the lid. "It was an ambush..." Her throat was thick with emotion and burning with the acid from her

123

stomach. "Sofía is *Sal.* She's the leader of the Black Jacks and she's known we were here the entire time. She's been biding her time and waiting for an opportunity to strike!"

Horror coursed through Archie as he stomped into the bathroom and plopped down on the edge of the whirlpool tub to face her. His teeth were clenched tight in rage. "Did she hurt you?" He reached out, cupping her cheek, "She threatened you, didn't she?"

Lucy couldn't stop herself from whimpering. "She offered me a wager. Play a hand of blackjack or she'd kill you. There were gunmen waiting to take you down!" She drew in a shaky breath, "If I won the hand, I would walk away unscathed...but if she won, I'd have to join the Black Jacks."

"That cheating bitch!" Archie thundered, snarling angrily, "This won't stand, Lucy. I won't let them take you from me!" He snapped. "First thing tomorrow, I'm going down there and she will rue the day she was born!" Lucy's hands grasping his face stopped him cold and he felt as if the world tipped on its axis.

Fat tears slid down Lucy's cheeks, dripping off her nose and splattering onto the gorgeous gown she wore. "They'll kill you, Gabriel! And not just you but *Danny*, too. They will wipe the Devils off the map! But she said if I stay with them, they won't hurt you." She covered her face with her hands. "I can't risk it. I won't!"

Archie shook his head violently. "We can take them, Lucy! You don't have to go through with this." His desperation grew deeper as he watched her struggle against him.

"No!" Lucy bellowed. "I won't lose one more person that I love. I can't do it!" She pushed hard against his shoulder, craving a moment alone. She needed to compose herself. Lucy stomped away from Gabe and headed straight for the sink. She scrubbed her face clean of makeup. Brutally, she brushed her teeth and used the entire mini-bottle of mouthwash the hotel had provided for them. Lucy swept her ebony hair into a bun before reaching back, trying to undo the zipper on her dress. She tugged and toiled until she felt Gabe's warm fingers at her back, easing the zipper down her spine. The minute the dress came loose, she tore it off, balling it up and hurling it into the corner with the cut. Sadness was quickly replacing the anger that bubbled up in her gut.

Watching Lucy wrestle with invisible demons tore something open inside of Archie. He couldn't take it anymore. "Enough!" Moving in front of her, his hands slid over her body and he dragged her to him again. "I told you I could protect you. You have to trust me!"

"Sofía knew everything about us! She knew we got married in Errol and she was aware the second we arrived in Reno. She has eyes and ears everywhere. And I'm willing to bet her spies would be happy to get some blood on their hands if it meant getting into her good graces." Lucy peered up at him.

"I don't care what the fuck she promised you! I won't go home without you!" Archie cried.

"What do you even care?" Lucy snarled. "When we go home, the only thing that's waiting for me is divorce papers, raising Danny, and putting up with more sexual harassment from the Devils." She drew in a ragged breath. "Do you think I'm not fully aware that I need a unanimous vote to join the MC? I will never get that, Gabe! Danny will never give me his vote, even if you somehow changed your mind." Her entire body was shaking. "This prospecthood was all a temporary situation you're planning on sweeping under the rug once you can kick me out on my ass." Lucy had one chance to make good and she wouldn't waste it. "I won't *ever* be able to help you as a Devil." Lucy chewed her bottom lip. "But as a Black Jack, I can save you…"

The muscle in Archie's jaw was ticking dangerously again, "I have always wanted more for you out of life than this. Don't you get it? It's why I fought so hard to keep you away. I never wanted it to come down to life or death, Lucy. I care about you too much to let it happen!"

"And I love you too much to let you die!"

Silence hung between Lucy and Gabe for a long time. He turned away from her, his gritty eyes closed tight against the anguish he felt. "You can't love me, Lucy."

"It's too fucking late! I already do." Lucy sagged under the weight of her grief. "In the morning, I will leave this hotel as a member of the Black Jacks and you'll go back to the Devil's Own." He fingertips trailed over his tensed muscles. "Tonight I want to forget everything that's happened in the last week. I want to spend the night in your arms. Just this once, let me be your wife."

Archie was weak. He'd loved Lucy since before he even knew what that really meant. His soul was irreparably tangled with hers now and he couldn't have denied her even if he wanted to. Archie's fingers brushed her cheek and slid to her chin, tilting her face upward. He could taste the salty tang of her tears against her flushed skin. Everything in the world was wrong, except for when their lips met in a searing kiss.

Lucy couldn't stand to be parted from him for another second. Gabe was the salve that her wounded soul needed. "I love you," she whispered between kisses, "And I know you love me too. This could be the last time we see each other. Don't lie to me, Gabriel."

There was a split second Archie contemplated lying. If he pulled this off, he could push Lucy away once and for all...but he was not strong enough to do it.

He growled. "I do love you, Lucy. I love you so much it hurts."

Tears rained harder down Lucy's cheeks as she tumbled into the throes of ecstasy with him. This time when they made love, both of their hearts were open completely. Tugging him against her, she reveled in the warmth of his body covering hers. Their first coupling was fast and furious—she needed to release the pain she felt. The second time, was slow and sensual. Lucy spent inordinate time memorizing every inch of him. She traced his lips, remapped his scars, and tangled her fingers in his hair. Lucy was determined to relive this moment with him every day for the rest of her life.

Archie's his mind turned with endless possibilities. He ached to experience every little miracle with this woman: buying their first house, bickering over renovation projects, planning a real wedding, giving birth to their first child...the Archer curse be damned. Somewhere along the line he'd fallen head over heels for his wife. It was the worst thing that ever happened to him. "Lucy—"

"Don't," Lucy begged. Burying her face in the crook of his neck, she closed her eyes tight against the pain splitting her heart. "There's no tomorrow, Gabriel. Only tonight. Just let it be..."

For once, he did.

Chapter Eleven

In the hazy grey light of dawn, Lucy disentangled herself from Gabe's arms. She hadn't slept a single moment last night and was running on adrenaline alone. Lucy was more exhausted by the fear of what was to come than the events of last evening. She remained silent as she stuffed the rest of her belongings into her bag. Reluctantly she grabbed the Black Jacks' leather cut from the bathroom floor, brushed it off a few times and eased onto her back. Lucy paused to press one last kiss to Gabe's lips. He was still pretending to sleep...she was infinitely grateful for that. Everything they needed to say had been said last night. To reopen those wounds now would be far too much to bear.

Lucy tossed her bag over her shoulder without fanfare and slipped out the door. She kept her gaze level as she inhaled the thick desert air. It was her very last breath of freedom.

As promised, a car was waiting to take her away. Sofía sat in the back, her hands folded across her lap regally. "No tears." She smiled darkly. "Good."

There were no more tears left, no more emotion left inside Lucy. She was cold and empty except for regret. That meant only one thing: she was officially a Black Jack now.

* * *

Archie placed a gruff call to Kyle, Hunter, and Mort to inform them he'd be arriving in town sometime in the afternoon. He'd also tasked them with summoning the club for a meeting immediately upon his return. It was their responsibility to make sure every available member with voting privileges was sitting in that War Room when Archie arrived. The only person they weren't to contact was Danny…

Daniel Harding was Lucy's only family and he deserved to know what had happened before it became public knowledge. Of all the things Archie was dreading, telling Danny was number one on the list.

The drive back seemed brutally long. Although Lucy had slept most of the trip to Reno, knowing she was resting peacefully beside him had been oddly comforting. Her soft breathing and the occasional murmur kept Archie smiling; he avoided cursing out other drivers so he wouldn't disrupt her sleep. Without her presence to temper him, Archie was the worst combination of fuck-all tired, pissed off, and floundering to breathe under the crushing weight of his fear. He drove like a maniac, pushing hard to get back to Errol as soon as possible.

Danny was standing out on the lawn when the van screeched down the street. He had clearly just gotten out of bed, his sweatpants resting low on his hips. Obviously, he'd lost his shirt a while ago and couldn't be bothered to find it again. Scratching his shaggy blonde head, Danny pushed back the messy locks and jogged to the passenger side. When he found the seat was empty his face fell. "Where's Lucy?"

"Danny—" Archie leapt from the van, hurrying to explain before Danny lost his temper. He was too late.

"WHERE THE FUCK IS MY SISTER?" Danny went from lax to raging in two seconds flat. Stalking around the car, he grabbed Archie by the lapels of his vest and slammed him against the van. When Archie didn't fight back, Danny's terror deepened. "What the hell happened out there?"

"I need you to listen to me," Archie begged, guilt crushing him and pushing him closer to the edge of drowning in his grief. "I'll explain everything inside. Come on." Dragging Danny through the unkempt grass, Archie kicked aside mail and papers that hadn't been picked up in quite some time. As soon as they walked in, there was an odor of burnt food mingled with the acrid stench of garbage. Archie was almost glad Lucy wasn't here to see how badly Danny had wrecked the house. "Sit down."

Danny shook, knocking aside several dirty plates as he plopped down on the couch. His fists were balled up and his teeth were clenched so tightly it seemed as if his jaw would crack. Danny leaned slightly forward to catch every word as Archie began to speak.

"Shit went south, man…" Scrubbing a hand over the stubbled curve of his jaw, Archie exhaled sharply. "The Black Jacks we used to know have changed. They're women. Run by this bitch Sofía—"

"You got beat by a group of *chicks*? Dude, what the fuck!" Danny hollered. In his mind, men were the stronger sex and he saw no way how Archie could've lost. His blood suddenly froze in his veins. Danny knew how badly Lucy wanted to join up with the MC. His breath hitched in his throat. "Wait, did she do it on purpose? Did Lucy decide to join up with them?"

"No! There was no choice. Lucy traded her life…for mine." Archie had trouble choking out the words. The emotion was thick in his throat as he watched Danny struggle to digest the information. "The Black Jacks ambushed her and gave her an ultimatum: join up or they'd kill all of us. I told her we'd fight it but…you know Lucy."

Yeah, he did. She'd rather sacrifice herself than let anyone she loved get hurt. Danny's breathing grew ragged as he descended into a cursing fit that lasted several minutes. Eventually, the end of the violent rant was punctuated by a very forceful, *"Fuck!"*

Archie nodded along the entire time, clearly in agreement with Danny's summation.
"We can't just leave her there, man! I don't give a fuck what she said. I swore an oath on the day my

parents died to *always* protect her." Danny's eyes grew damp and he rubbed at them. "I've let her down in every other way. I can't do it again. Not this time!"

Archie pulled Danny into a tight hug. "I swear on my fucking life, we will get Lucy back. The Black Jacks will rue the fucking day they ever messed with the Devil's Own." That seemed to placate Danny for the moment. "Get dressed. The whole crew is assembled and awaiting instruction. I'll take you over to the clubhouse."

Half an hour later, Danny and Archie entered the War Room. Applause and hollers of joy at the return of their fearless leader were quickly halted when they saw the state he was in. It took every shred of Archie's self control to explain everything they'd learned while in Reno. Whispers and angry curses erupted when the rest of the crew learned the Black Jacks had taken Lucy. Unfortunately, no one could seem to agree on a course of action and conflict broke out shortly thereafter…

"Should we even go after her at all? She isn't *really* a Devil. There's no rule against a prospect choosing to patch with another club. It ain't like they're torturing the girl! They made her a full member and welcomed her into their ranks. I personally don't see how that warrants a dangerous, potentially bloody, rescue mission…" PJ Murphy was a soft-spoken, levelheaded Southern gentleman. He had a way about him that put the world at ease and was universally liked by his peers...until now.

Archie's jaw clenched tightly as he glanced around the table. Several other members seemed to be nodding in agreement with what PJ was saying. Danny was on the brink of losing control but Archie got there first. He slammed his hand on the table to silence the rumblings. "Lucy isn't just a prospect with this club. She's my *wife*!"

It was in that moment Daniel Harding realized his best friend was in love with Lucy. He fully intended to deal with that later, but right now there were more important things to do. Danny pointed an accusatory finger at PJ. "If this was your *mama* being taken by the Black Jacks you wouldn't hesitate for a second. Lucy's the only family I have left. She's my sister and we *are* going after her, with or without you!"

Voices erupted again, bickering and sniping at each other. The cacophony of noise rose until Archie could take it no longer. "Enough!" He grabbed the gavel and slammed it down so hard that the wooden mallet cracked right in half. Archie paused, composing himself before he spoke again. "We'll adjourn for fifteen minutes then come back and vote on this *anonymously*."

"Why anonymously?" PJ pressed, his face molded into a mask of confusion.

"Because if you vote to leave Lucy in Reno and I find out about it, I'm going to *kill* you," Archie snarled back. "Now get out of my sight!" Pinching the bridge of his nose, he kept his eyes shut tight as the rest of the club filed out. Archie expected that when he opened them again, everyone would be gone. Instead, he found himself face to face with Kyle. "Now's not the time, kid."

Kyle shifted nervously. "I know I can't vote because I'm a prospect..." Archie was giving him the *'get to the fucking point'* face and he willingly obliged. "But I won't stop fighting until she's home safe. I'm with you a hundred percent and that goes for Mort and Hunter, too. I don't give a fuck what PJ says. Lucy *is* one of us. We won't let her go without a fight." Archie clasped Kyle on the shoulder in silent gratitude before ordering him out of the room a second time.

Per his duties as treasurer and ombudsman to the club, Big Mike removed the ballot box from a locked closet in the corner of the War Room. The founding members of the Devil's Own MC were ruthless smugglers and gangsters, but they certainly had an appreciation for beautiful things. The Devil's insignia had been hand carved into the expertly crafted box and fashioned with a hinge that was rumored to be made of solid gold. Traditions ran deep here and, in situations like this one, it was comforting to know there was still order in the world.

Big Mike cleared his throat. "Boys, grab a pen and a piece of paper from one of the prospects. Voting will begin now." Big Mike gave Archie a wide berth as he stepped out of the room once more. Slipping his glasses on, he cast his own vote before instructing members to place their papers in the box one by one.

Danny bounced in anticipation as he stood at the back of the line with Archie. There were fourteen members assembled and given the nature of the vote, no proxies would be accepted today. They only needed eight votes to win… but when Danny started counting the men in line, he was quickly discouraged.

Archie and Danny's votes had were two in favor of saving Lucy. Monster looked distraught enough to vote for his sister's safe return. Beaver's face was still busted up; he would either vote to save Lucy in fear of Archie's wrath or against her to spite Archie for decking him. Wilson and PJ were engaged in a heated discussion that Danny couldn't quite make out…but he was sure it meant the worst.

One by one the men filed in: PJ Murphy cast his ballot first followed by Wilson Stevens, Harold "Hal" Cline, Gerry McLean, Nico Newman, Grayson Thomas, Timothy "Rager" Andrews, Luis Demauro, Nathaniel Aaron, Terence "Beaver" Cantor, James "Monster" Walcott, and finally Daniel Harding. These were Archie's brothers by choice; he had grown to know them very well over the years. It felt wrong that they were all at odds now…

Archie strode in the War Room and placed the final vote into the box.

"That's it for the voting," Big Mike called out. With that, he closed the War Room door behind him and locked it to avoid distraction. Two of the prospects stood guard, ensuring that the count was fair and accurate, though everybody knew Big Mike walked the straight and narrow.

Mort already had shots waiting when Danny approached the bar. Archie slammed back three shots of tequila with no chaser before Danny tugged him back. "You aren't the sloppy drunk, Archie. I proudly hold that title. So, cool it."

Archie did not want to *cool it.* He wanted to numb the pain swirling inside him. God only knew what the hell kind of torment Lucy was being subjected to right now. Sofía Salma was a twisted bitch and his imagination ran wild with possibilities. It was too much to bear. "How fucking long does it take to count fourteen votes!" He thundered.

The door to the War Room opened moments later and Big Mike stepped out. Silence filled the entire clubhouse as he cleared his throat. "The decision to go after Lucy and the Black Jacks has passed…unanimously."

Danny left his position at the bar, running around to hug every single member tightly. Several of them trying to fend him off but he didn't even care. Lucy would be rescued and that was all he needed to know. "Yes!" Danny pumped his fist in the air.

Archie slumped down on a bar stool, breathing a sigh of relief. His club was behind him wholly and completely. It was more than he ever could have asked for. When he looked up, PJ was standing there with a slight smile on his face. "Thank you," Archie murmured.

"Don't thank me just yet. I know you want your wife back but we can't go off half-cocked. We need a plan of attack. Based on what you told us, the Black Jacks are smart, organized, and they've got connections. I think we need to tap our sister charters in California and Louisiana. Maybe they're willing to get their hands dirty," PJ replied. "I also know you want to get to her as soon as possible but they're going to be expecting retaliation right away. We need to sit on this for a little while, shore up our defenses, and hit them when they're least expecting it."

Danny moved to argue but Archie cut him off. "You're right," Archie agreed. "If we go out there now, they will slaughter us like sheep. We don't know who we're dealing with yet." Archie drew in a shaky breath. "Lucy's a smart girl. She can hold her own until we get there." He straightened his spine, and turned to address the group again. "All those in favor of calling in our other charters?" The *aye*

138

echoed through the room. It was settled. They were going to get Lucy back, no matter what it took.

* * *

The shimmering black sedan pulled up to a massive compound approximately an hour outside the city. Sofía swiped her ID card and wrought iron gates creaked open to admit them. Lucy immediately felt as if she'd entered a prison. Thick concrete walls at least thirty feet high stretched above them were accentuated by barbed wire laid over the top. There were guards pacing with guns and talking to each other on two-way radios. Sofía must have sensed Lucy's discomfort because she smiled. "Don't worry, *mija*, this is only to keep us safe inside. You are free to come and go as you please. Security will issue you your very own keycard once you get settled in."

Lucy didn't believe that for a single second. The minute they stopped, she was ushered through the front of the building into a room that looked like it had been ripped out of a mausoleum. Thick white marble columns supported a ceiling that seemed to stretch to the sky. Natural sunlight filtered down onto the sparkling floor made of the same marble as the columns. Along the walls were paintings from various artists and judging from the frames alone, Lucy was pretty sure they were originals. The entire place oozed decadence, wealth, and death.

Even though it was the dead of summer, Lucy shivered. The air conditioning cooled her skin and mingled with the uneasy feeling swirling in her gut. Gooseflesh erupted over every inch of her and she rubbed her arms briskly. They continued down a long, sparse hallway that led into an antechamber filled with metal bunk beds. If this wasn't a prison, she didn't know what the hell was. Sofía seemed to read her mind.

"This is an area reserved for our sisters visiting from out of town. I've also opened it as a place for battered women and children to seek refuge," Sofía explained casually. The harder Sofía tried to convince Lucy she was some kind of saint, the less she believed it. There was something fundamentally wrong about this entire place, starting with the woman who ran it.

The hallway twisted and led to a corridor punctuated with dozens of simple white doors. Sofía slithered down the corridor, until she reached the end. She knocked several times before pushing the door open. "Our new members share their rooms," She explained before flinging the door open. "Cecclia, this is Lucy."

Lucy nodded a greeting to the woman who was hunched over her bed, reading from an ancient bible. Cecilia looked to be around Lucy's age— though like Lucy, she was hardened by violence. A thick curtain of dyed blue hair fell in waves over her shoulders, shielding the left side of her face from view. Cecelia's rough hands were wrapped around a rosary of crystal beads.

"Cecelia!"

"*Atrévete, puta*!" Cecelia snarled like a caged animal, the bible falling from her hands. When she moved, her hair fell away from her face, revealing a crescent scar marring her caramel skin. Cecelia's back was tensed and she looked ready to lunge at any moment.

Lucy tossed her bag on the empty bed. She sniggered softly at Sofía's indignation, watching the older woman struggle to keep a lid on her anger. "You heard her, Sofía. I think it's time you leave." She didn't need to speak Spanish to know Cecelia had told Sofía to get lost in the rudest way possible. Lucy definitely agreed; she was sick of Sofía's smugness.

Sofía's spine straightened and a flash of anger twisted her face. "Perhaps your new friend can show you the rest of the place, then. I will see you later, Lucy." Turning on her heel, she swept from the room and didn't bother to stop the door from slamming behind her.

Lucy and Cecelia were left alone and silence hung between them awkwardly. Lucy glanced around, taking stock of the place. There were twin beds on opposite sides of the room. A clean set of sheets and towels had been placed on one bare mattress. In the corner there were matching dressers with a small area to hang items up. Along the back wall were built in desks separated by a bookshelf in the

141

middle. Lucy had never been to college but she expected this was what a dorm room would look like. It wasn't the worst place Lucy had ever seen...but it certainly wasn't home.

Cecelia stared at Lucy while she unpacked. The girl hung up a few things before folding the rest and shoving them in drawers. Cecelia smiled when Lucy tore off the Black Jacks cut, balled it up, and threw it in the bottom of the closet. Setting the bible aside, she extended her hand, "Cecelia Santos. *Cece.*"

"Lucy...Archer. I would say it's nice to meet you but judging from the major Jesus vibe you're putting off, I'm guessing you would prefer I didn't lie." Lucy shook Cecelia's hand cordially before she went to put the sheets on the bed. "How'd you end up here?" There was a long silence and Lucy wondered whether or not she understood. Lucy turned to face Cecelia again. She chewed her bottom lip uncertainly. "Do you speak English?"

"Of course I speak English!" Outrage spread over Cecelia's features. "Stupid bitch...you got to stay quiet. God's always listening." She stalked over to the bookshelf and grabbed another bible. Pushing it into Lucy's arms, Cecelia's expressive grey eyes narrowed dangerously. "If you want to survive here, you need to accept Christ into your heart and study his words." She glanced around, tilting her head toward the wall.

Paranoia speared through Lucy as she looked around. This woman was off her rocker! "Uh, yeah thanks, but I'm not sure I can deal with any bullshit about this being God's plan right now." Still, she set the book on the nightstand and kicked off her boots. The white linoleum floor was icy beneath Lucy's feet and she hopped onto the bed. Cecelia rolled her eyes and dropped a few choice curses before going back to her studies.

Lucy made up the bed and hung her towel in the small bathroom they shared. After a while, boredom settled in. There wasn't anything else to do, so she grabbed the bible and flipped it open. Cecelia looked over at her and Lucy had an epiphany. Cecelia wasn't a religious nut; she was trying to teach Lucy how to communicate without getting caught in here. "You know, on second thought…I could definitely use a little bible study." On all the pages of the bible there were numbers scribbled. It was code…hopefully a fucking brilliant code that could be their ticket out of this hellhole once and for all. Cecelia and Lucy shared a private smile before a bell tolled ominously throughout the compound. Lucy was immediately on high alert, "What the fuck is that?"

"Lunch." Cecelia stood from the bed and grabbed her own cut from its position on the floor of her closet. "Come on, we don't have all day. I'll introduce you to the rest of the girls." Tugging her blue hair away from her scarred face, Cecelia looked significantly fiercer. "*Vámonos*!" She commanded.

143

"Alright, alright, keep your panties on." Lucy followed Cecelia's lead and tossed on her cut before following her out into the hall. Something told her that despite Cece's prickly nature, they would be close friends. Survival was all that mattered and making alliances was the way to do it. One way or another, Lucy was going to get out of here…it was only a matter of time.

Chapter Twelve

Lucy's stomach growled as they entered the massive dining room. She didn't realize how hungry she was until this moment, surrounded by the delicious smells wafting from a cafeteria-style kitchen. She followed Cecelia through a sea of tables until they reached a row of trays. Lucy grabbed an apple, a sandwich, and a sinful-looking piece of German chocolate cake before she thought better of it. "This stuff is safe to eat, right?" Cecelia rolled her eyes and grabbed the apple from Lucy. She took a large bite before letting it drop back onto the tray with a bang. Lucy stared down at the apple, frowning markedly. "You could have just said yes…"

Cecelia helped herself to a slice of pizza and grabbed a couple bottles of water before leading Lucy over to a table. Plopping down unceremoniously, she motioned for Lucy to take the seat beside her. "Welcome to bible study."

Lucy suddenly felt like she was back in high school as four sets of eyes stared her down. "I'm Lucy

Archer." She introduced herself, hoping that they would a little more accepting of her than Cece was.

An effervescent redhead who was scribbling in a notebook looked up and gave a little wave. "I'm Julia Amos. And this is my sister Candice Rey. You might expect us to have the same last name since we're sisters but—"

"She doesn't need our fucking life story, J," Candice cut her off. Unlike Julia she was blonde, though both sisters shared the same warm brown eyes. "Call me Candy, everybody does." She ignored the death-glare Julia was giving her and popped a cherry tomato into her mouth.

"As I was saying," Julia cleared her throat. "The girl to your left is Adela. She doesn't talk."

Lucy peered at the girl sympathetically. Adela couldn't have been more than seventeen and the expression on her face never wavered from terrified. Lucy knew exactly how she felt. She nodded, prompting Julia to continue with the table rundown.

"Beatrice Patton—"

"Bea," Beatrice had a thick Irish accent. Her blonde hair was tied in a tight bun to keep it out of her face. Her eyes were soft and blue, softening her otherwise brutish appearance. She took a long sip of tea and leaned back. "Keep your head down, nose clean, and avoid conflict. Best way to avoid trouble. You'll get used to the way things work around here, we all did."

"Look, this is all great advice but I really want to know why the fuck you're all still here. Sofía said we're free to come and go as we please. Besides the layout of this massive compound being confusing, I don't see what's stopping me from walking out of here and going home…" Lucy probed.

A low gasp of shock ripped through the table. Except for Cecelia, who snorted and slapped her hand down on the table. "Walk out the front door? Why didn't I think of that?" Tapping her ripped, scarred cheek with her index finger, she feigned a ponderous pose. "Oh, right! That's how I got half my fucking face torn off. Walk out the door she says…" Cecelia descended into a string of curses in Spanish.

"Is there a problem here, ladies?" A shrewd, sour-faced woman leaned over the table. "You must be the new girl." She leaned in closer to Lucy. "I'm Priscilla." Her pug nose wrinkled as she faked a smile. "I'm so sorry you got stuck at the freaks and geeks table. Why don't you come sit with us?"

Lucy shook her head. "Thanks. I'm okay here."

Priscilla's expression soured. "You should probably know that Cecelia's last roommate ended transferring rooms after she *bit* her."

"Better move along then, *puta*. I get a taste for human flesh sometimes and you're lookin' real good today." Cecelia gnashed her teeth, causing Priscilla to scoot away in fear. "That's right, move your ass!" Turning back to her meal, Cecelia took a large bite of pizza. "For the record, I only bit her because she tried to go through my stuff. I'll bite you too, if you try it…"

"Irina needed *twelve* stitches," Julia piped up. When Cecelia scoffed at her, Julia raised her hands in mock surrender. "I just thought she should know all the information. Geez!" She went back to picking at her salad.

Lucy's appetite waned as she stared down at her sandwich. It tasted fine—great, even—but knowing for sure she was a prisoner here made her sick to her stomach. Cecelia was covering her scarred cheek as if she were embarrassed. Uncomfortable silence hung between them. Lucy looked around at all the women coming and going. Her curiosity prompted her to break the tension. "How many people actually live here?"

"Couple hundred, in total," Julia replied and adjusted her glasses. "Although the population fluctuates based on how many refugees we have at any given time." She licked her lips and lowered her voice to a whisper. "Recently I've noticed a lot of new members coming in. Sofía is preparing for something and I'm willing to wager it's bad news."

"Shut up, Julia!" Candy hissed, "You say something like that and you're going to find yourself in big trouble around here. Gazing around the room, she was fairly confident no one had heard her sister but she still refused to relax. "Come on, it's time go." She picked up the rest of Julia's salad and hurled it in the trash.

Bea shook her head. "Aw, leave her alone. It's nice to have somebody around here who isn't a raging bitch all the time." She took another long swallow of tea. "But I should get going too. I've got work in an hour." When Bea got up, Adela followed her to the opposite side of the dining hall.

Lucy and Cecelia were the last to leave. When they returned to the room, both women got out their bibles and Cecelia started to show Lucy the code they used to pass secret messages to each other. Lucy had never seen anything so complicated in her entire life. "Where the fuck did you come up with this?"

"I'm an electrical engineer," Cecelia replied.

Snorting softly, Lucy looked up at her and realized she wasn't kidding. "Oh, you're *actually* an engineer." Cecelia was a strange, maybe rabid, genius.

"I did all the electrical work in this building, *chica*. I'm not just a pretty face, you know." It was how she knew the compound so well and why they were so desperate to keep her on the inside. "Keep reading. When you get to the end of Numbers, wake me up. I need a nap." Crawling into her bed, Cece tugged the blanket up to her shoulder and turned her back.

Lucy stared down at the bible verse and the alphanumeric code that Cecelia had devised. She was supposed to be concentrating but her thoughts slipped back to Gabe. What she wouldn't give to feel his arms wrapped around her right now… Lucy's heart ached fiercely.

Flopping onto her back, Lucy rested the bible on her abdomen as she stared up at the ceiling. Did he miss her as much as she missed him? Did he miss her at all? After a while, Lucy's exhaustion caught up with her and her eyes fluttered closed. Dreams of Gabriel filled her head and in sleep, tears flowed down her cheeks.

* * *

Archie rubbed his temples and tried to block out the voices volleying across the War Room table. "Alright, enough!" His voice was hoarse from yelling. "We've been at this for *hours*. Our brothers from Cali will be arriving soon. Maybe they'll have some better ideas." They were all hungry and tired after hours of brainstorming. Archie had sent the prospects to Marge's to pick up some food a while ago; they were due back any time. Big Mike recommended they sleep in shifts in case any of their brothers showed up from out of town. The only person who wasn't

149

eating or resting was Archie...he hadn't done much of either since leaving Reno.

Danny stepped into the War Room and closed the door behind him. Tossing a burger and fries in Archie's direction, Danny plopped down beside him. He opened up his own meal and dug in heartily. "You want to talk about it?" He asked through a mouthful of burger.

"No." Archie let out a rumbling sigh. If Lucy were here, she'd have torn Danny a new one for his disgusting table manners. But she wasn't. She was alone in Reno and he was stuck here, feeling guilty.

"Well, that's too fucking bad." There was a beat of silence and Danny dropped his burger, wiping his greasy fingers on his jeans. "I've heard the story of your trip more times than I can count. What you failed to mention is at what point you fell in love with my little sister."

Archie was in no mood to fight Danny and too exhausted to lie. Instead, he met Danny's gaze. "What do you want me to say? I love Lucy."

Danny scrubbed a hand over his stubbled cheek. "You son of a bitch..." His perfect, delicate, sweet little sister may have been twenty-six years old, but in Danny's eyes she was still the bucktoothed kid forever chasing his heels. "How long has this been going on?"

"I didn't even *kiss* her until after we were married! I swear to you, I have the utmost respect for your sister." Archie put up his palms in mock surrender.

"Why did you say it like that? You didn't even…" Danny let out a horrified gasp, "You *banged* my sister?" Danny leapt from his chair and grabbed Archie by his cut. He forcefully slammed him down on the War Room table, cursing and spitting in anger.

"Get off me!" Archie thundered, pushing Danny off and tugging his leather cut down to smooth any wrinkles. "Lucy is my *wife*!" Archie drew in a ragged breath, "You want to know the truth? I've loved Lucy since I was a kid. I was fucking terrified of what I felt for her." Collapsing in his chair, Archie exhaled sharply. "So, I pushed her away because I didn't want to lose Lucy *and* my best friend. But you know what, Danny? I'm done pretending. I want to wake up with her every morning. I want to have kids with her. I want to grow old and hold hands on some fucking porch somewhere *with* Lucy." He felt his stomach tighten painfully. "But right now? All I want is to get her back."

Danny was quiet for a long moment before he took his seat again. Stuffing more food into his mouth, he chewed thoughtfully before he spoke. Danny glanced over at Archie and sighed. "I guess if there's anyone that's good enough for her, it's you."

"What's the catch?"

"If you *ever* hurt my little sister, I don't care that you're my best friend or that we grew up together or that you're the President of this club. I will hunt you down and I will tear you apart piece by piece. Then I'll feed your carcass to coyotes!" Danny's face darkened menacingly.

Archie felt a sense of relief wash over him. "I swear on my life, I won't hurt her." Unfortunately, he already had...but he planned on making it up to her when he got her back.

Danny nodded his acquiescence. "Good. Now get your shit together, man. You have to stop walking around here like a zombie. You moping around and sighing all the fucking time is not good for morale. Pull it together, eat something, and then you're taking the next sleeping shift. You hear me?" He glared across the table. "If Lucy were here, you know she'd agree with me." It might have been a low blow but manipulation was all Danny had at this point. Archie was off the rails.

He opened up his own meal and took a small bite of the burger. At this point it was cold and the bun was soggy but it was sustenance. Archie and Danny finished their meals in relative silence. Every once in a while Hunter or Mort would pop in to see if they needed anything to drink or another burger. Danny was halfway through his third when the cavalry arrived.

Marco Caraway was the President and leader of the California branch of the Devil's Own MC. In addition to his high ranking position within the club, he was also Lucy's godfather and a very good friend to the Hardings. Marco was in his early fifties and greying just slightly at his temples; there was a joviality that seemed to elevate his handsomeness. On this occasion, his face was drawn and pale. It was clear he was a man on a mission.

"You've been riding for hours, Marco," Archie clasped his hand and shook it tightly, "Take a load off. Can I get you something to eat?"

"No," Marco's voice was grave. "I rushed out here as soon as I heard about Lucy." He let out a shaky breath. "When we spoke on the phone yesterday, I started putting all the pieces together. Lucy isn't the only woman who's been taken."

Archie offered Marco a seat and poured him a hearty snifter of brandy. At the very least, he could use a drink; the man was shaking like a leaf. "What are you talking about?"

"Our brothers to the North, the Redhawks? Their girl Julia was taken a few weeks ago, same night as Candy," Marco pressed. His stomach twisted painfully at her name passing his lips. Even though their relationship failed years ago, she would always mean the world to him. "And Los Santos? One of their patched members, Cecelia, disappeared over a year ago without a trace. She was out near Reno

153

doing some freelance engineering work. Turns out, it was for a shell company owned by Sofía Salma. When you told us she's the one running the Black Jacks, everything started clicking into place." His lips pursed into a tight line. "I even spoke with the Nightriders…"

Archie's eyes widened in shock. "Are you out of your damn mind? You could've started a war!"

"Narayan Bosko's daughter Adela went missing too. She's seventeen years old, Archie. He came at us weeks ago, accusing us of taking her!" There were very specific rules the Devil's Own followed and harming women and children were not tolerated. Even the Nightriders knew that. Marco planted his feet firmly and crossed his arms over his chest. "I don't care if the man is a monster, *nobody* deserves to lose their child."

Marco was right. Old feuds meant nothing right now. There more important things at stake. "Sofía Salma is taking them and using them to keep us in our place." The threat of hurting the women they loved was enough to keep them at bay. She was counting on their anger and hostility to keep them down but Archie had a better idea. "Get Narayan on the phone. I'm going to call Rogelio and the Redhawks." He faced the group. "Sofía is counting on the fact that we've been divided for so long. It stops today. Separate we're weak, but together we're strong enough to take her down."

Danny cleared his throat. "The Nightriders, the Redhawks, and Los Santos may be willing to play nice to bring Lucy and the rest of our girls home but what happens after that? It could turn into a bloodbath!" He licked his lips. "If you're going to do this, we need some kind of insurance."

"So we'll write up a treaty," Archie suggested. "We need to figure out voting rights so everybody gets a say. This is still a democratic club." He sighed. "We need someone to draw it up..."

"How about Anita?" Danny piped up. "She's a judge or some shit now. I bet she could come up with something that would make sense. You know damn well she's helped us all of out a bind at some point. She's a friend to this club."

Stalking to the door, Archie leaned his head out. "Mort!"

The heavyset, bespectacled prospect jogged over. "Yeah, boss?"

"I need you to go into town and find Anita Raleigh. Tell her Lucy is in trouble and we need her help." Mort was halfway out the door when Archie called out to him again, "And Mort? Persuade her, *don't* strong-arm her. I won't have people accusing the Devils of threatening Errol's citizens. You hear me?" Mort nodded swiftly before heading out. Archie heard his bike flare to life and he rode into town.

155

With that taken care of, Archie turned to Marco. "Let's get this shit show on the road."

* * *

An hour later, Rogelio Santos, Narayan Bosko, and Tim Gunter had all agreed to come to Errol to negotiate the terms of their agreement. Archie sent Kyle to make sure the bed and breakfast was set up for the leaders and Hunter cleared the motor lodge for their entourage. Once everyone arrived, the population of Errol would more than double overnight. It was about to get very crowded in this tiny town…

Mort returned shortly thereafter with a very flustered Anita Raleigh. She quickly readjusted her skirt, tugging it down and trying to smooth the wispy strands of strawberry blonde hair that had come loose from her bun. "I hear you need some kind of legally binding contract written?" She shifted her briefcase, grinning widely.

Archie turned to face her and his eyes widened. "God damn it, I told him to persuade you, not knock you around!" There were traces of bruises along her throat and his anger grew tenfold. "I'm going to kill that little son of a bitch."

Anita stepped in front of Archie before he could stop her. "On the contrary, Mort was extremely persuasive. I was *very* impressed." Her blue eyes sparkled with mirth. "Let's focus on the task at hand, shall we? I understand Errol's about to become a neutral territory for several rival clubs. So, you need a contract that everyone will be amenable to but will still allow you to make decisions in the event of an emergency." Her lips curved up at the corners. "I'll need a copy of your most recently updated charter."

Archie would now have to scrub the mental images of Mort and Anita from his brain...but least she was happy, he supposed. Anita hummed to herself as she commandeered the small office off the back of the bar. Mort stayed close by, fetching her coffee and guarding the door so nobody bothered her. Every once in a while he'd grin like the cat that caught the canary. It was incredibly disturbing.

"Well that's an image I'll never get out of my head," Danny muttered to himself. He slapped Archie's shoulder and prodded him toward the back. "Things are settled for the moment. Everyone's been mobilized. Marco sent the rest of the prospects out to get some essentials. There's nothing more you can do tonight. So, you're going to bed. End of story."

Archie stifled a yawn. "Yeah, you're probably right." If Lucy were here, he'd have been in bed hours ago, though they wouldn't be sleeping. A rumbling sigh emanated from his chest. Archie kicked off his cowboy boots and tossed his cut over the back of a chair. Archie wanted to rest but his mind continued to race. For hours he tossed and turned, thinking only of Lucy and how she must be feeling right now. Even after he succumbed to sleep, nightmares caused him the thrash until he startled awake again, just as exhausted as he'd been before. There was no rest for the wicked tonight...

Chapter Thirteen

"Hey, Sleeping Beauty! Get your ass up!" Cecelia shook Lucy's shoulder several times. "What the fuck is the matter with you?" Although Cecelia was her usual hardass self, there was a note of worry in her voice. It had been almost three weeks since Lucy arrived and Cecelia had been watching her slip further into darkness. Lucy was barely eating and when she did, it was thrown up a few hours later. Something was wrong and Cecelia would be damned if she sat back and did nothing. "Don't make me dump you off that bed, *chica*!"

Lucy groaned and rolled onto her back. "Cece, can you please back off? I feel like shit." She threw her arm over her face, to shield her eyes. "I didn't sleep well last night." Hell, she hadn't slept well in weeks. Lucy wanted to blame it on stress or missing Gabe but there was something else nagging at her. Something that would change everything...

Cecelia scoffed derisively. "No!" She snapped. "Get up, take a shower, brush your teeth—for the love of God— and stop feeling sorry for yourself!"

"I don't feel sorry for myself!" Lucy sat up a bit too quickly and her vision swam. She gripped the side of the bed tightly. Nausea churned in her veins as she

158

fought against the urge to vomit all over Cecelia's combat boots. Breathing raggedly, Lucy desperately tried to control the churning in her gut.

Stepping back quickly, Cecelia got out of the line of fire. "Shit..." Her demeanor went from angry to sympathetic in a heartbeat. "Stay put, I'll be right back."

Lucy couldn't have gone anywhere if she wanted to, not when she was as weak and nauseated as right now. Cecelia returned a few minutes later with a cup of hot tea and several packages of crackers. Laying them down on Lucy's bed, she sat opposite her. Lucy accepted the tea gratefully and inhaled the sweet peppermint scent. Opening up the crackers, she nibbled on a corner before washing it down with a hearty swallow of tea. She repeated the action several times before she felt strong enough to address the issue at hand. "I'm not wallowing, Cecelia." Lucy's hand slid over the still-flat plane of her belly and she exhaled sharply. "I think I-I..." Her voice cracked painfully. "I'm pregnant."

Cecelia unloaded a string of curses and dragged her fingers through the dyed strands of her blue hair. "Are you sure?" She leaned forward. "I mean *really* sure?" This changed things. The group was slowly but surely working on a way out of this place. With Lucy's natural leadership abilities, the pair had gotten more accomplished in the last month than she had alone in over a year. They'd even figured out a way to debug the bunkroom so they had a safe place to meet. Cecelia had high hopes if they stayed the course, they'd be out in a few months. But if Lucy was really pregnant, they didn't have months to wait...they had to get out *now*.

"I'm late as hell, I'm nauseous all the time, I'm exhausted..." Lucy pushed herself up from the bed and paced the length of the room. She took another sip of tea and sighed. "If this gets back to Sofía, there's no telling what she'll do. We just need to keep working." She grabbed a fresh set of clothes.

"What are you doing?" Cecelia asked, grabbing Lucy's arm tight as she walked past. "You can't just unload this on me and walk off!"

Lucy smiled grimly. "A good friend told me I needed to shower and brush my teeth. Then I'm going to see how well this damn security pass works. We're *allegedly* free to come and go as we please. I'm going to test that theory. It's time we figure out what we're really up against."

Cecelia paled. "You want to end up with your face ripped off?" She suddenly felt a rush of protectiveness toward Lucy; nothing was going to happen to her while Cece was around. "Did you learn nothing from my mistakes?"

"You walked into the front hall, stole a gun off a guard, and tried to bust out. I'm going to try a different approach," Lucy soothed. "Trust me." A thought passed over her and Lucy turned and walked back to the desk. Leaning over it, she scribbled a few lines on a piece of paper and folded it several times. "If I don't make it back, there's something I need you to do..."

"I do not like this, Lucy!" Cecelia snapped. "If we get the group together and I get more done on mapping the compound, we can probably move up our timeline by at least a couple weeks."

"First I need to determine if this is even something we need to worry about." Pressing the note into Cecelia's hand, she narrowed her gaze. "I have a brother. His name's Daniel Harding...if I don't get back, I need you to give this to him. He'll understand." Lucy rested a hand on Cecelia's shoulder. "*Promise* me, Cece."

There was a note of reluctance in her posture but Cece agreed nevertheless. "Yeah, I promise..." Cecelia hated all of this. She let go of Lucy only because kicking the ass of a possibly pregnant chick wasn't on her to-do list today. In light of this new information, she had to rally the group and get them to increase their patrols. Julia got a position in commissary and had been slowly gathering food and gear. Bea continued to work in medical and was pilfering supplies as best she could without anyone noticing. Candy's job was logistical. She was clocking all the guard shifts and had made friends with a couple of the higher-ups who ran things. Lucy, though...she was the brains. Cecelia wasn't sure how they could do this without her.

Lucy showered and hurried through her routine, ignoring the gnawing in her gut. Her curly hair was still damp as she tossed her purse over her shoulder and headed toward freedom. She said nothing to the guards as she headed down the West hallway and straight for the front door. To her surprise, no one said anything as she swiped her access badge. The massive doors to the outside swung open and she inhaled the scent of the desert deep into her lungs.

Keeping her head down, Lucy stalked outside. The whole time she was just waiting for a shot to the back or someone to stop her. She almost sobbed with relief when she found her Harley parked in a space near the front. Sliding her fingers over the pristine cherry red paint, she tossed her leg over and prepared to flee.

"Looks like we both had the same idea." Sofía's voice stabbed through Lucy's subconscious mind. Lucy nearly groaned; she had been so close, and yet so far away. Sofía moved to the left, leaning against a custom bike with the Black Jack's insignia emblazoned on the side. "Mind if I join you?"

"Yeah, I do, actually," Lucy replied curtly. "I've got errands to run. I don't need a chaperone."

Sofía's gaze darkened. "I have done nothing but offer you a brand new start. You are respected here. You are not treated like a second-class citizen or as a burden to the club. No one questions your right to ride!" She sighed, "If you would just let me, I could teach you so much, Lucy."

Toying with the key in the ignition, Lucy scoffed. "You don't get it, do you? Gabriel may be overbearing and yeah, he's a jackass sometimes...but he's *my* jackass." She pointed an accusatory finger at Sofía. "You took away my chance to change things with the Devils. You stole my life from me!"

"I *saved* your life!" Sofía roared, her cool façade suddenly slipping. All at once, the monster behind the mask was revealed. "Do you think I know nothing of this world? My father ran with a group of bikers in California. My life revolved around the club since the day I was born. My mother was a slave to my father's demands. Although they took vows, he spent every night in a different woman's bed, tarnishing the good name of our family. He used my mother like a piece of trash, keeping her pregnant until her body gave out...and when she finally died, he found another woman and did the same thing to her. My sisters and I...we swore things would be different."

Sofía's entire body was vibrating like a wire about to snap. "When I met my husband, he was soft spoken and sweet. I did not think he could be cruel or ruthless until the day we met my sister's fiancé." The haunted look in Sofía's eyes bled from her soul. "How could my Hector who loved me dearly and doted on our daughters be so unmoving?"

Against Lucy's better judgment, she listened quietly. Bloodshed and hatred between rival MCs was a tale as old as time. What the hell made this story different?

"I had three children with Hector. Magdalena was the oldest and so beautiful. She was a gentle soul. Paloma was the middle child, bright and happy. She could have cured cancer. But my little Teresita was my husband's pride and joy." Sofía's green eyes were bright with tears. "When she was two years old she got a terrible fever that wouldn't break." Her breath hitched in her throat, "On the way to the hospital, my family ended up in the middle of a war for territory. They forced my husband off the road. Teresa was shot through three times and Paloma died in the car accident. Hector was beaten so severely that his legs stopped working. He survived, somehow…and although his body was weakened, the hatred that raged inside him only grew stronger."

Lucy instinctively rested a hand over her womb. Although she wanted to feel no sympathy for Sofía, it crept over her nonetheless. "No one should ever have to go through the pain of losing family like that but the Black Jacks are not innocent either. They gunned my parents down in the street too. For *no reason!* Just because they could!" She shook her head forcefully. "I still don't know why you're telling me this."

"I am getting there, *querida*. Patience." Sofía seemed to rally and the tears were banished beneath her icy exterior again. "Hector changed after that. He was distant and cold. He became bloodthirsty, cruel, and reckless." Sofía frowned. "Magdalena grew up watching her father try to commit suicide every day." She straightened her shoulders.

This story was getting longwinded and Lucy's patience was wearing thin. "Your life is tragic. I get it, but I didn't volunteer to hear your entire life story. You have two minutes to make your point and then I'm out of here. I'd like to get my errands accomplished before sundown."

Sofía remained quiet for a long moment. "Time passed and Hector drifted further away. I wanted to rekindle a relationship with my family, most especially my sisters…" She swallowed hard. "Roberta welcomed me back with open arms but Louisa and Maya were not so forgiving."

Lucy tried to ignore the uneasiness that crept over her. It could have been a coincidence that every summer they would spend months visiting with her mother Louisa's sisters Roberta and Maya. Those names were common enough…

"I regret very much that I did not try harder." Sofía smiled sadly. "If I had, I would've gotten to know you. I swear on the grave of my mother, I did not know what Hector had planned. If I knew my sister would be caught in the crossfire…"

"What are you saying?" Lucy's anger spilled outward like molten lava, mingling with her shock. "You're my…"

"*Tía*, yes." Sofía filled in after Lucy trailed off. "You were named after our mother—Lucia. I see so much of her and Louisa in you." Tears burned in her eyes once more. "When I found out you had joined with the Devil's Own, I had to do something!" She cried. "Men are violent, cruel creatures. We are better off without them! My husband, your father, *your* husband, they are monsters! They perpetuate violence and hatred. Look at how they try to control you. How your husband treated you!" She slipped from her bike. "I am offering you a partnership, Lucy. You are a kindred spirit. A natural born leader…already in a few short weeks you have garnered a reputation for being someone our people can trust."

"I won't be your puppet!" Lucy cried. "I get it, Sofía. Your father was a dick and your husband wasn't much better. I'm sure Gabe's appearance can be frightening to some but he is honorable, dependable, and sweet." She glanced away. "I love him."

Sofía did not seem convinced. "Men are the root cause of all the violence, depravity, wars, pestilence, and fear in this world. You think that you love him because you do not know any better." She inhaled sharply. "In the new world I am building, there will be peace, love, joy, abundance to share. We will not be weak any longer, *mija*."

Lucy gritted her teeth. "I'm not weak *now*. See? I'm getting the fuck out of here." Having had enough for one day, she kicked her bike into gear and took off like a shot. The gates opened automatically from the inside and there was only one road out of the place. Lucy took it all the way to a two-lane highway and followed the signs toward a small town between Reno and the Black Jack compound. Her mind spun as she mulled over Sofía's confession. Could it possibly be true? Lucy wished her mother were still living...there were so many things she needed to talk to her about right now.

Eventually, Lucy found herself in the middle of a town. There was a diner, a post office, a small clothing shop, and, the last building on the left was a tiny family-owned pharmacy. Pushing open the door to the shop, Lucy threw money down on the counter as she grabbed a pregnancy test from the shelf. She hunkered down in the small bathroom and stared at the box until her vision practically blurred. The instructions were easy: Open box, piss on the stick, and wait. If only it easy enough to gather her confidence. Lucy's hands were shaking the whole time and she narrowly avoided dropping the test into the toilet. It had been a long time since she had something to pray for but in that moment, she begged for the strength to turn the test over.

Seconds ticked into minutes and Lucy knew it was time. Gripping the plastic stick tighter, she stared down at the tiny plus sign staring back at her. Emotion clogged Lucy's throat as she stuffed the stick into the garbage can and washed her hands until her skin was raw. Stomping out of the bathroom, she headed for the front.

"Miss, are you all right?" The cashier looked up at Lucy's pale, drawn face.

"I need to borrow your phone."

"I'm not sup—"

"Give me the goddamn phone or I'm going to come over this counter and break you in half!" Lucy warned menacingly. And by God, the way she felt at this moment, she might have gone through with it. Thankfully, neither of them had to find out. The girl handed the phone over and Lucy pulled a scrap of paper from her pocket. After she dialed, she held her breath until a masculine voice picked up on the other side. Lucy didn't let him get a word in edgewise. "I need you to meet me at the bar in an hour...you know where?"

"Lucy?"

"Just be there!" Lucy hung up. Stalking out of the pharmacy, she took a shaky breath. After composing herself as much as possible, she headed toward the city limits. Darkness was starting to fall but she didn't care. This mattered more. Her unborn child mattered more. Even if it meant fighting dirty.

* * *

Errol was overrun with bikers.

Anita frowned as she sat on her porch, listening to the thunderous rumble of engines in the distance. The machine hum could be heard all day and all night now. Between Los Santos, the Redhawks, the Nightriders, and the Devil's Own from out of town, there was always someone motoring around town.

The lodge was way over capacity, the bed and breakfast housing the MC's most important leaders was booked solid. Even rooms at the clubhouse were occupied. It had taken the prospects half a week to clean out the mess Danny had made at the Hardings but now that it was done, Archie and Danny holed up there. Even with that accomplished, there were still MC members without a place to go and the prospects were forced to take the overflow into their own homes. Everyone was on edge. Disaster was imminent. No one felt that more acutely than the people who called Errol home…

Winding her way through the backyards of friends and neighbors, Anita stared along the pathway she'd spent the summers running. She could almost picture Lucy standing out on the front porch, Danny chasing after her with threats to feed her to a garden snake; Archie pretended to play along but Anita knew he would have protected Lucy at any cost. Not all that much had changed, she supposed.

Anita climbed the stairs to the Harding's back door and rapped sharply. A train whistle blew in the distance and she turned away just long enough for a pair of strong arms to wrap around her waist. She cried out, sending a sharp elbow into the faceless assailant's stomach.

"Anita!" Mort's breath was knocked out of him as she lashed out. "Shit, it's just me!"

Anita whirled around, her neat braid snapping around like a whip. Her expression bordered on murderous. "I hope you learned your lesson, Mortimer Lally! You don't sneak up on a woman like that, especially with every biker in three states hanging around here!" Her hands rested on her hips as she frowned at him sternly but it was really hard to stay mad. Mort looked so apologetic. His big blue eyes were soft and sorrowful as hung his head in shame.

"I wasn't thinking. I'm sorry…" He leaned in, nuzzling her neck before he pressed a soft kiss to her cheek. "Make it up to you later?" Mort stole another kiss—this time on the lips—and he smirked as she leaned into it. Wrapping his arms around her waist, he gazed lovingly into her eyes. "You shouldn't be here, pumpkin. There's too much going on. Go home and I'll come by later."

"Damn right you will," Anita huffed and allowed the barest hint of a smile to cross her features. "But I'm not here for you. I need to speak with Archie and Danny."

"I don't think that's the best idea." Mort lowered his voice. "Danny's a wreck. Archie had to knock him out last night because he wanted to go off after Lucy himself. It's been real nasty lately. Everybody's on edge…"

"Well, it's a good thing I'm here then." Anita rapped sharply on door and waited with her arms crossed.

Archie was in the middle of yet another *How I Met Your Mother* rerun when he was dragged out of his thoughts. Lumbering to the door, he was poised to give Mort the verbal lashing of his life. The man was loyal, Archie would give him that, but he was a klutz. Mort had tripped over his own shoelace and nearly knocked out his own front teeth in front of Rogelio Santos two nights ago. It wouldn't do to have anyone thinking his club was made up of people who couldn't even walk without taking a nosedive. When he realized it was Anita on his doorstep, uneasiness crept into his chest. "Don't tell me you're here to arrest somebody."

"I'm a judge, not a cop." Anita pushed her way inside and headed into the living room. Danny was snoring loudly and she turned to Archie, "Vodka?"

"Allergy meds…I put them *in* the vodka. He's been out for a while. I can tell he's not dead because people four streets down can hear him snoring." Archie pulled out a kitchen chair and motioned for her to sit. "I appreciate you helping us out with that treaty, Anita, but I'm not in a position to return any favors right now."

"I don't need any favors. I'm here because I got a call from an old friend of mine…well, my ex-husband, actually." Anita cleared her throat. "That's a long story…but anyway, Steve told me he got a call from a girl he met at a bar. Said her name was Lucy Archer and she's trying to get the fuck away from the Black Jacks."

Archie's legs felt weak and he stumbled to the table. "Steve Ellis? Short, WASP-y looking bastard?"

"That's the one," Anita grimaced. "Lucy contacted him to look into some family records. Errol's such a small place that most of our records are handwritten and stored down at Town Hall." She paused, lacing her fingers together before she spoke again. "Louisa Calaveras married Edmond Harding in 1983. According to one of the documents, Louisa had five siblings, two brothers who passed early on in life. But there were four girls: Maya, Roberta, Louisa…and Sofía."

"Sofía? As in…" Archie felt his stomach turn over.

"Sofía Calaveras married Hector Salma several years earlier…" Anita pressed. "I did some digging and it's true, Archie. The woman you're going after is Lucy and Danny's aunt." She sat up straighter. "You don't have to worry that storming the Bastille will cause tension, though. Lucy also mentioned she wants to prosecute Sofía for fraud, extortion, kidnapping, and assault."

"Assault?" Archie's chest tightened painfully, "Did that bitch hurt Lucy?"

"No, but apparently there is a girl named Cecelia whose face is all scarred up after she tried to escape the Black Jacks' compound." Anita patted Archie's hand. "Steve said that the meeting was brief. They communicated using handwritten notes in case someone was listening in…she's doing okay, Archie. She's strong."

Archie let out a breath he hadn't known he was holding. "It's going to be a few more days. I just need Tim and Rogelio to agree on their entry points into the compound. From what we've learned, their headquarters are a fortress." He frowned, "The White House doesn't even have that much security. They've got guns, tear gas, grenades…and a whole shitload of guards." He rested his palms on the table. "I got my boys their Christmas presents early. Every one of my members has a bulletproof vest."

"I hope you got them for the prospects too." Anita stared down her nose at him.

173

"Anita—"

"Don't you '*Anita*' me, Archer! It is not every day you meet a man who's sweet, caring, and who also knows how to please a woman in bed. If that big lug does not come home to me because you cheaped out and refused to buy three more vests, I will bury you in so much red tape that your club will never open its doors again!"

Archie made a face. "That was way more information that I needed…" He muttered. "*Fine*, I'll order vests for the prospects." That seemed to satisfy Anita for the moment. She stood up and headed for the door. Reaching out, Archie grasped her wrist. "Hey, thank you for bringing this to me. I didn't realize the lawyer was *your* Steve."

Anita smiled sadly. "He hasn't been *my* Steve for a long time." She tugged her jacket tighter around herself because of the slight chill in the early September breeze, not because she needed comfort… "I told him to look out for Lucy and keep his mouth shut about this. I don't want anyone to know Lucy's related to this bitch."

Danny leaned in the doorway, shirtless and still drooling slightly in his sleep. "Related to who?" He scratched his belly and chest aimlessly, his pants drooping low on his lips. They were in significant danger of sliding right off his slim hips and Anita had to force herself to look away. "What's going on?" Danny yawned.

Anita decided it would better to defer to Archie on this one. Danny was in a very fragile state right now. Without Lucy to keep him in line, Danny was falling apart. Scurrying to the door, Anita glanced back. "You boys have a good night. I'll be expecting my prospect home before midnight, you hear?"

"Yes, ma'am," Archie drawled and chuckled to himself. He'd let them have their fun.

What wasn't going to be fun was telling Danny the truth about his mother's side of the family. He debated back and forth telling Danny about Sofía but seeing how lost he looked was the deciding factor. Archie would continue to reassure Danny his sister was fine and look after him until they brought her home safe. "You want something to eat? I'm getting pretty good at making hotdogs."

"A monkey could make hotdogs," Danny huffed. "No, I'm not hungry." Flopping down at the table, his forehead plunked onto the tabletop as his consciousness waned again.

Archie flicked off the television and headed down the hall. His childhood bedroom was completely unchanged. There were still rocket ship sheets on the bed, though they had been laundered so many times the little shapes seemed melted. His old, crinkled Harley Davidson poster hung lopsidedly on the wall above a small blue dresser. The room was cozy and quiet...but it's not where Archie wanted to be.

Instead, he padded into Lucy's room and sat down on the edge of her bed. She was a no frills kind of girl and her room reflected that. The walls were painted light beige and unadorned—except for a picture of her mother taped to the mirror. Sentimental items dotted her armoire. The whole place was infused with her presence.

Archie lay down, resting his head on Lucy's pillow. He inhaled the delicate scent of her shampoo lingering on the pillowcase. The confirmation she was still alive and kicking comforted him. For the first time in weeks, Archie actually felt as if he could relax. He fell asleep there, spread out on her bed, and dreamed of nothing.

Chapter Fourteen

Bea checked Lucy's blood pressure again, releasing the cuff with a rush of air. "Your BP is in the toilet. It's no wonder you feel like shit." Pressing a hand to Lucy's pale cheek, her frown deepened. "You're not drinking enough." Stalking over to the fridge, she rifled around until she came up with a sports drink and plopped a straw into it. "Small sips to start."

Julia was sitting cross-legged on a table next to Candy, nervously chewing her thumbnail. "Is there something we can do?"

"These things pass in time," Candy assured her. "It's totally normal."

Lucy ignored the crushing ache at the base of her skull; so far, nothing had alleviated the nausea that roiled inside of her. The best she could do was grin and bear it. "Candy's right. I'm fine, Jules." Lucy took a sip of the proffered drink and tried not to gag at the saccharin taste of it. Everyone was watching her and so she choked down another swallow before sitting up. "Look, women have been doing this for millennia. I'm pretty sure I'm not the first one to have a little morning sickness. So, let's get back to the task at hand."

"Luce is right," Cecelia replied curtly. "We've got bigger problems. Sofía hasn't been spotted in a few days. Last time she disappeared, she came back with Lucy. This is her pattern. I think it's safe to assume she's got another girl on her radar…"

"We've got a small window of opportunity to bust out of here. There's no telling when she's going to come back. There's no time to lose." Lucy moved to stand up but her vision swam again and Bea pushed her back against the bed before her knees buckled. Lucy dragged a deep gulp of air into her lungs. "Shit!"

Bea shook her head forcefully. "Lucy is in *no* condition to be running around right now." She folded her arms. "I'm putting my foot down. She

177

needs *at least* a day or two of rehydration and rest. And that's if she doesn't have any further nausea and vomiting, which is unlikely given how she's been feeling. Any undue stress could complicate the pregnancy and I'm not willing to risk it. Are you?" Bea faced Cecelia—who was frowning and muttering curses under her breath. "You wanted my professional opinion and there it is. Take it or leave it."

Silence hung between them for a moment and Lucy gathered her strength. She was the weak link; it wasn't fair to hold them all back. "Go without me."

"No!" Julia squealed. "We can't!"

Cecelia shushed Julia and held up a hand before Candy could jump in. "Listen to me!" She stood up straighter to emphasize her point. "If the five of us get out, we can go to our own clubs for help…"

"You really think Los Santos, the Nightriders, and the Redhawks are going to sign on help the Devil's Own?" Candy snorted. "Are you out of your freakin' mind?"

Cecelia rounded on her. "Los Santos have no beef with the Devils."

Adela had not spoken a single word since she arrived. She shifted several times before clearing her throat. Her timid voice was scratchy from disuse. "The Nightriders will put aside their blood feud to see that I am safely returned. My father is an honorable man. He can be trusted to help."

Lucy wrapped an arm around Adela and held her close. She couldn't imagine how frightened the little girl was; it only validated how important this was. What they were doing was the right thing. "That takes care of the Nightriders." She peered over at Julia and Candy. "The Redhawks are friendly with the Devils. My godfather is Marco Caraway."

"Marco is Candy's *boyfriend*," Julia giggled.

"He's *not* my boyfriend!" Candy's cheeks reddened. Marco was fifteen years her senior, not that it mattered. She'd been infatuated with him from the moment they met. They shared a couple crazy nights years ago...she'd ended it abruptly when she realized she cared a hell of a lot more than he did. Marco never called her again, proving she was right all along. More importantly, Marco didn't know about the son they shared and Candy wanted to keep it that way. If there were any other way, she would've suggested it right then and there... Unfortunately nothing came to mind. "So, we bust out of here, rally the troops, and then come back for Lucy and the rest of the girls who want out of here?"

Julia bobbed her head. "It could work!"

"I also have a contact in Reno who could be helpful." Lucy reached into her pocket and pulled Steve's card from her pocket. "This guy knows how things are here and is willing to take a risk. If Sofía realizes you're gone, the first place she's going to go is to your clubs. She won't be expecting you to have a contact on the outside. Steve can be an asset."

Cecelia grabbed the crinkled card and frowned. "You think some pansy lawyer is the answer?" She shook her head. "For all we know, he could be a spy for Sofía."

Lucy supposed that could be true, but her instincts told her Steve could be trusted. "So, we make sure our bases are covered. Errol is a couple hours drive from here. Get into town and my husband will help you." She could tell Cecelia wasn't convinced. "Archie is the President of the Devil's Own. He's got the power to put any plan you want into action. If you're worried, Danny's my brother. He can be a bit of a prick sometimes but he's one of the good guys." She reached out, grasping Cece's shoulder. "He will do anything in his power to get me back." Just saying his name made Lucy's soul ache. "Split up. Candy and Julia can go to Steve. Cece, Bea, and Adela will go to Errol. That way, if something goes wrong, the other group can still get help for the rest of us..."

"How sure are you that this will work?" Julia didn't look convinced.

Four sets of eyes stared Lucy down. In turn, she shifted her position. "Going in opposite directions will confuse Sofía's security detail. This is your best shot."

"Julia should go with Bea. Adela, Candy, and I will go to Errol," Cecelia suggested. Julia was a sweet spirited girl and Cecelia didn't getting caught in the crossfire if things went south in Errol. Candy could hold her own and nobody would hurt Adela while Cecelia was around. It was the best option for everyone.

"I'm in." Bea grinned.

Adela nodded her consent swiftly.

"Me too," Candy replied for both her and Julia.

"Then it's settled." Cecelia turned to the assembled group. "Candy, I need you to sneak into the guard booth. Grab the keys to a couple of the vans. Bea, we'll need the medical stock you've been able to collect. Julia, bring your stash back here too. We'll divvy it up." Her jaw was grimly set. "Meet back here in twenty minutes." The group hurried out, rushing to perform their duties. Lucy and Cecelia were momentarily left alone. "Are you sure about this?"

Lucy forced a smile. "I would only slow you down, Cece." She paused, collecting her thoughts before she spoke again. "You remember that note I gave you for Danny? I want you to give it to him when you get to town. Archie is the rational one. Danny is a bit of a hothead. He'll want proof that I'm alive before he hears a single word you're going to say."

Cecelia was throwing items into her bag. She mulled over Lucy's request. "I'll give him the message but I don't want you to think for a second we ain't coming back. We don't leave our own behind." Moving toward Lucy, Cece grabbed her shoulder. "You hang in there. Take care of that baby and don't worry about anything else."

Lucy hugged Cecelia tightly. "I will." Although Cecelia and the rest of the group would be breaking out, it was Lucy who had the hardest job of all. She had to cover for them. The longer she was able to keep up appearances, the better chance the girls had of escaping without notice. "Be safe."

"I promise." Cecelia pulled away from Lucy just as the other girls began to filter back into the room. Julia arrived first with a bunch of items from the commissary. Although it wasn't much, each girl was issued a Swiss army knife and several candy bars, matches, and a flashlight. Bea made up packets with sterile gauze, saline, alcohol swabs, surgical scissors, tape, and some bandages. Meanwhile, Adela had drawn everyone maps of the layout and Candy scribbled in the guard shifts and which doors it would be easiest to sneak out of. With very little effort, Candy had also obtained the keys to a couple of transport vans.

It took all of Lucy's strength to ignore the nausea that churned in her veins as she said her goodbyes to each of the girls. "Keep your head down. It'll all be over soon," She urged. Lucy said a silent prayer this would work. One way or another she was going to get out of here; she just hoped for the baby's sake, it wasn't in a body bag.

* * *

Steve paced the length of his office, one hand wrapped around a mug of coffee and the other resting against the gun strapped to his hip. The muscle in his jaw ticked in aggravation as he replayed the series of events that led him here. It had been seven long years since his alcoholism ended the most meaningful relationship in his life. Anita Raleigh had such a vibrant spark; he couldn't help but fall for her. She left a tiny town in Nevada and travelled three thousand miles to study pre-law in Boston. Although she knew no one and felt terribly out of place in a bustling city, she braved it like a champion. Watching Anita flourish under pressure was the most amazing thing he'd ever seen. How could he not fall in love with her?

Sophomore year, they moved in together and Steve couldn't imagine spending their lives apart. Even though it was reckless and stupid, they eloped before law school. Steve and Anita bought a little apartment on the wrong side of the tracks. Money was tight and that's when the fighting began...instead of turning to his partner for support, Steve hit the bottle. The drunker he was, the less he cared about his actions and the meaner he got. Anita stayed far longer than he deserved, begging him to get help every step of the way. Steve was stubborn and unyielding…and eventually Anita gave up.

Somehow he'd tricked himself into believing she would never leave. When she finally did, the consequences were devastating. Steve spent a few days wallowing but then made the decision that his wife was more important than the booze. It took him several months to get sober. He planned on making the trek to Nevada and winning Anita back…when suddenly this case dropped into his lap.

Taking down the Black Jacks was Steve's shot at making something of himself. But the assignment was dangerous and living undercover was no place for the woman he loved. It would be cruel to ask her to give up everything she'd worked for, especially for a husband who had squandered their love and treated her so poorly. So, Steve made a choice…and now that the end was in sight, he was starting to realize how much he regretted it.

Brushing away thoughts of the past, Steve stepped away from the window and padded back to his desk. Seven years of photos, eyewitness statements, and encounters with the Black Jacks. His background in law made Steve the perfect candidate for this assignment. He was organized, thorough, and driven to prove that Sofía Salma was the worst kind of criminal. Her dirty fingers were stuck in dozens of different pies: embezzlement, fraud, trafficking of drugs, and she had a cache of military grade weapons in her arsenal large enough to get her charged with treason. Steve also couldn't discount the kidnapping, assault, and extortion allegations either.

"Heads up, boss, there are two unidentified parties entering through the Eastern door," A voice broke through Steve's churning thoughts.

Tugging his suit jacket on, Steve shoved his badge into his pocket. "Nobody moves except on my command. You hear me, Reynolds?" He shoved the file into the desk and it locked automatically. Heading through the front door, there was a moment of silence before Bea and Julia burst through the glass doors. He drew his gun, holding it steady. "Were you followed?"

Bea pushed Julia behind her instantly, gritting her teeth as she stared him down. Her accent seemed to grow thicker when she was angry. "No, now drop the gun…" Her hand slipped down to the army knife that Julia had collected from the commissary, ready to draw if necessary. Bea's surprise was palpable when the man removed his hand from the gun and grinned at her.

"You're Lucy's people?" Steve felt a fluttering of hope in his chest once more; he was so close to cracking this case wide open he could practically taste it. Seven years of work. Seven years of pain and heartache and failure…seven years of putting his life on hold. "Reynolds, Flanagan," Steve barked, "Secure the perimeter. Anything on the monitor, Dennis?"

"No sir, we're all clear," Dennis replied from the opposite side of the room.

"Alright," Steve took a step toward Bea and Julia. "I'm sorry about that." Opening up the door to his office, he motioned to two chairs. "Where are the rest of the girls? Where's Lucy?"

Julia moved to sit but Bea grabbed her to keep her from getting too comfortable. Bea was not yet convinced they were safe. "I've never met a lawyer with this much security." Peeking around the doorjamb, Bea never released her grip on the knife. "What's your deal?"

"I'm not going to hurt you." Steve softened his gaze. "I just need to take precautions. You know how Sofía is. I'm not taking any chances."

Bea perched on a chair, narrowing her eyes dangerously. "It was Lucy's idea to split up the group. We were instructed to come here." Bea wasn't about to tell Steve where the other girls were going. "For some stupid reason, Lucy thought we could trust you."

"You *can* trust me," Steve smirked at Bea's distrust. "Let's start over, alright? We haven't even been properly introduced. I'm Steve Ellis, Esquire...and the head of the FBI operation that's been working to take Sofía Salma and the Black Jacks down for good."

"FBI?" Julia echoed and her eyes rolled skyward. "I should've known you were a cop!" She folded her arms over her chest, more defensive than she'd been since they arrived.

"Do you have something against cops?" Steve raised an eyebrow at her.

Julia opened her mouth but Bea cut her off swiftly, "We've got work to do here. Lucy's still at the Black Jack compound and we don't have the time to be dicking around."

"What do you mean Lucy's still in there?" Steve gritted his teeth. Lucy was the reason he was back in touch with Anita; she was the reason he was this close to cracking this case. Not to mention, Lucy was pregnant. It was all the more reason to get her out of there as soon as possible. "Where is the other half of your group?"

A silent correspondence volleyed back and forth between the two women, debating what information should be shared. Bea finally nodded but Julia was the one who spoke up, "The rest of the group headed for Errol. Lucy's husband heads up the Devil's Own out there. Adela and Cecelia believe they can get Los Santos and the Nightriders to join forces. Candy is going to get in touch with Marco and see if the Redhawks would be open to an alliance."

"He doesn't need to know all that," Bea pressed.

Steve began furiously taking notes. "The more I know, the better I'll be able to help." He paused and glanced at Julia. "I can tell there's a reason you don't trust law enforcement. Believe me, I used to be just like you…" He licked his lips, "But I'm here for one reason and one reason only, and that's to put Sofía Salma behind bars."

The conviction with which Steve spoke seemed to calm Julia down because she exhaled sharply. "I still have the map Adela made of the compound and Cecelia's entry and exit points. Plus, Bea knows the medical wing better than anyone." Glancing around the room, Jules noticed several boxes stacked against the wall that she assumed were relevant to the case. "May I?"

"Help yourself." Steve pointed her in the right direction and the two of them delved right in. It didn't take long before they became lost in strategizing and coming up with creative ways to break into the compound. Bea smiled knowingly as she slipped from the room in search of coffee. Steve and Julia were lost in their own little world. All previous hesitations seemed to fly out the window.

* * *

Cecelia jammed on the brakes as she pulled off onto the only road into Errol. "Hey, wake up," Cece snapped, startling Candy out of a very peaceful sleep. Adela had copiloted the entire way, which gave the other girl a chance to finally rest. Now that they'd reached the border, uneasiness crept into

Cecelia's chest. Up ahead there was a barricade set up and a several scouts meandering around. Reaching into her pocket, Cece grabbed her knife and held it tightly as a blonde boy with a crew cut stomped toward the window.

Kyle's fingertips wrapped around the gun strapped to his waist as he knocked on the van's window. With four different motorcycle clubs and every MC leader who was worth their salt being in town, it was unanimously decided that the borders needed to be locked down tight. Errol was a small town. Everybody knew everybody else and that meant strangers stuck out like a sore thumb. Whoever was in this van, they definitely weren't one of the locals. "If you're looking for a shortcut, you need to go around. Borders are closed."

Adela shifted uncomfortably, tucking her legs beneath her and wrapping her arms around her chest. Candy rested a comforting hand on her shoulder to soothe her. "Cece, you need to keep your cool. They're probably just afraid of Black Jack retaliation. Keep it calm."

"I'm always calm." Cecelia snarled and rolled down the window. "We're here to see Archie." She might as well have told him she wanted to see the Wizard of Oz; the boy's expression was cold and blank. "*Now*," Cece added, for good measure.

"Step out of the car." Kyle's hand wrapped tighter around his gun. This woman was very abrasive and

189

when the streetlight hit her face, he could see she was deeply scarred along the left side of her face. Something seemed off with her and he wasn't taking any chances. "*Now*." He parroted.

Cecelia's jaw tightened in anger. "You either get Archie here or I'm going to fuck you and this barricade up, *pendejo*." She could see he was reaching for his gun and she launched herself out of the car, tackling him to the ground. There was a shout of angry voices behind her as she wrestled the gun away from Kyle and stood up, pointing it blindly at anyone who dared come near her. Cece whirled around, looking for an exit point but there were twelve barrels pointing at her. There was no escape...Cecelia was outgunned, outnumbered, and there was only one way she could see this going down. She cursed a blue streak and put her hands up in defeat.

"Cecelia?"

The voice sounded so familiar but...how could that be? When she turned, her heart nearly stopped. "Ramón?" Cece cried.

Candy slammed the van door open. Adela suddenly took off like a shot, tears burning down her face as she leapt into the arms of the tallest man in the group. The massive man in a Nightrider's cut dwarfed the tiny girl; he hugged Adela tightly as she sobbed unintelligible words into his shoulder.

"What's going on here?" Candy slipped out of the van, her eyes wandering over the group and her heart suddenly stopped. She glanced over at the prospect that had addressed them first.

Spitting blood, Kyle dragged himself from the ground. He glared daggers at Cecelia, wishing that she wasn't playfully joking with Ramón Diaz—third in command of Los Santos. Any other day, he'd have dished it out as good as she'd given it to him. Instead, Kyle turned his attention to Candy. "You're one of them, aren't you? The girls who were taken?"

Candy's chest ached with anxiety. Men from every club were milling around, chatting amongst themselves. She exhaled shakily, ignoring Kyle's question. "Is *Marco* here?"

Kyle's brow furrowed, "Yeah. He's at the bed and breakfast. Are you—"

Horror ripped through Candy as she staggered away from him. "I need to get out of here. Call Archie *now*!" Candy's only thought was of her son...the son Marco didn't know they had. "Cece! Adela! Let's go!"

"What's got your panties in a wad?" Cecelia raised an eyebrow. Candy didn't answer, glaring harder instead. Shrugging it off, Cece took charge again. "Alright boys, there will be time for shooting the shit later. I need Rogelio and the rest of *los Presidentes* at the Devil's Headquarters pronto." She turned back toward Kyle with a lazy smile that was intended as an apology. "Make it happen."

Kyle fired off a text to Archie and got an immediate response telling him to bring the girls to the clubhouse. Rogelio, Narayan, Tim, and Marco were on their way as well. Kyle led Cecelia back toward the van with a quick set of directions. Even though she was clearly not happy with him, she got back into the van without argument and took off down the road.

Within five minutes the girls were being admitted into the gravel parking lot of the bar. Cece was blown away as she walked past men from every club, wearing their colors with pride. "They're here...they're *all* here..."

"I never thought I'd see the day..." Candy stayed close to Cecelia. She looked green as she came face to face with Marco. It took every ounce of strength in her body to avoid his steely gaze.

"Daddy!" Adela launched herself up the stairs and into her father's warm embrace. There were so many emotions rushing through her at the moment that she could hardly breathe. Bosko Narayan seemed to beam with pride, tears gathering in his warm brown eyes. It was the first time any of them had seen the man do anything more than grimace and frown.

Archie's heart twisted up in his chest as he took a step forward. "Where's Lucy? Where is my wife?" He pressed, stepping closer to Cecelia. The long silence that hung between them made him feel weak in the knees. "Is she—"

"*No*." Cecelia stepped forward, her scarred visage seeming illuminated in the pale light of the bar. She heard a wheezing gasp from beside her and she bit her lip, "I'm fine, *hermano*," Cece comforted Rogelio. She turned to face Archie without fear. "Lucy chose to stay behind..." She contemplated telling Archie about the baby and how Lucy sacrificed herself to help them but decided against it. It was not her secret to tell. "She made it possible for us to get out safely." When she turned, there was a lanky man standing outside the bar, his face was twisted into a scowl. Cece realized right away that there was a slight resemblance between Lucy and him. "Are you Danny?"

Danny had been kept fairly sedated, whether it was Archie's cold medicine cocktail or whatever booze he could get his hands on. When the woman addressed him, he blinked twice before her words registered. "Who's asking?"

"*I'm* asking," Cecelia fired back. "Lucy wanted me to give this letter to her brother, so I'm looking for him. Are you Daniel Harding or not?"

Danny's attitude changed immediately. "Give it to me!" He could hardly breathe he was clenching his body so hard. Closing the distance between them, he reached for the letter. "Please…"

Cecelia placed a hand on Danny's arm and slid the letter into his hand. "Hey." She seemed softer suddenly. "She's going to be fine. Lucy is a fighter." There was a moment of quiet solidarity between them.

"What's it say?" Archie probed, eager to know what his wife had to say to *Danny* but not him. A pang of jealousy stabbed through him before he could stop it. "Come on, don't keep us in suspense!"

Danny tore the letter open and read silently. His heart pounded as Lucy's words came to life on the page. He swallowed before he began to read aloud: "Danny, I keep thinking about my fifth birthday. One of the kids at my party pushed me down and got dirt all over my dress. You got in trouble for beating him up and were sent to bed with no cake. I snuck upstairs and brought you some anyway…" Danny's voice cracked painfully. "That night you made me a promise that you would always protect me, no matter what the cost. I think that may have been the cake talking but all these years later, you have always held up your end of the bargain. No matter what happens, I want you to understand that you never let me down. Please look after Gabe the way you've always looked after me. He's going to need your support now more than ever. Gabe will always be family, please remember that. I love you. Take care of yourself. Lucy." Danny didn't bother to wipe the tears streaming down his face as he rounded on Cecelia. "What the fuck is this? You said she was okay!"

Cecelia grabbed the letter from his hand and frowned. "Damn it! Stupid *puta* is trying to say goodbye like we aren't going to fucking break down the walls and get her out of there!" She drew in a ragged breath. "I don't care if I have to give up my life to do it." She turned to Danny and grasped his shoulders tightly. "Don't get yourself worked up. Lucy is family now and I won't rest until she's safe."

Archie felt his stomach tighten painfully. "Why would she write something like this?" He turned to face the scarred woman and he licked his lips. He'd somehow lulled himself into a false sense of security. The Black Jacks wouldn't hurt Lucy...right? Looking at Cece now, he was worried he'd misjudged the situation. "Did Sofía do that to you?"

"Sí," Cecelia replied softly. "A couple weeks after I arrived, I tried to escape...they had to bring out the big guns to stop me. She said it was an accident but I don't believe it for a second. That woman is unhinged. It took me months to recover. I almost lost my eye." Cece swallowed. "Just another reason we need to get moving. Lucy sent us here to find you. She hoped we could get the boys together to fight this side by side." She grinned at Archie. "You're way ahead of the game."

"With the Black Jacks holding our people hostage, we couldn't take any chances with fucking this up. You're too important…" Lucy was too important. Archie's grief was starting to bleed into anger. Why would Lucy stay behind? Why would she write Danny a goodbye letter like that? Why had she sacrificed herself for these strangers? Archie would give anything to get her back…anything at all.

* * *

Candy had done an excellent job of giving Marco the silent treatment, but when Danny and Archie went into the house the group began to disperse and she could feel his eyes on her. Shifting uncomfortably, Candy looked for a way to escape. She broke left, heading toward the van, but he was faster. Marco grabbed her arm before she could bolt.

"So…" Marco's face was contorted into a frown. "How long has it been, Candy?"

"Not long enough." Candy inched away from him. "If you'll excuse me—" She tried to turn away but he dogged her every step. The familiar scent of sandalwood and leather made her heart twist in her chest. "Seriously! What do you want, Marco?"

"I just want to make sure you're okay!" Marco snarled.

"What do you even care?" She fired back. "I haven't heard from you in fifteen years! Don't you dare stand there and act like you give a damn about me."

"Jesus, Candy…" Marco scrubbed a hand across his stubbled jaw. "*You* were the one who ended things between us. I don't have any resentment toward you for breaking things off, honey, but don't act like it was my choice!" Marco's brows furrowed.

Candy slumped, knowing that he was right but hating how badly she still cared for him. "I'm fine, okay? Julia went with Bea, I'm sure she's fine too." This time when Candy shrugged away from Marco, she made sure to put distance between them. Heading back into the house, she followed the sound of voices. Cecelia had settled at the War Room table with Archie, Danny, and the rest of the Devils. Candy ensured her seat was far, far away from Marco before inserting herself into the conversation.

Anita entered a few minutes later with Mort and Kyle in tow. "I've been in contact with Steve. He said that there are two women there who were part of the group who broke out of the Black Jacks compound?" A sigh of relief washed over the table. "I don't know all the details yet but it seems that Steve's got a further reaching influence than I realized." Her complexion seemed chalky and her voice shook. "That being said, the FBI is willing to compensate you for your cooperation in this investigation."

Archie half expected pandemonium to break out at the mere mention of the feds...but instead, silence reigned. He glanced around the room. "What do you think, boys, this could be our best shot?"

"I'm all for it," Tim replied. "My girl's still in there. I ain't takin' any chances." He rested his palm on the table. "With the feds behind us, we don't need to worry about somebody taking the fall if things go south."

"Marco?" Archie turned to him next.

"I'm in."

"You have my support, as well," Narayan offered.

Rogelio Santos was nodding in agreement.

Throughout the conversation, Danny's focus remained solely on Cecelia. He itched to move the dark curtain of her dyed blue hair away from her face and examine the scars in detail. It took all his concentration not to...he had to keep reminding himself Cece would probably kill him if she even caught him staring. Danny cleared his throat, finally deciding it was his turn to speak. "I don't give a rat's ass if the feds get involved or not. I will do anything to get Lucy back. She'd do the same for us..."

More murmurs erupted around the table. It was driving Cece nuts. "Enough! It's time for some action. We're wasting precious time." She turned to face

Rogelio. "Is this what you've been up to while I was rotting in there? Talking until you're blue in the face, going around in circles…"

Rogelio rolled his eyes. "You see what I have to go through with this one? She's got a mouth on her."

Danny simply stood up, tugging his pants up his hips as he went. "I'm with Cece on this one. I'm sick of *talking*. It's been weeks now. Lucy managed to break out a crew while imprisoned in that dump and we can't even get our fucking asses together to go after her? Enough dicking around!" Danny folded his arms. "Archie? Come on man!"

Archie dragged a hand over his face. "Fuel up, get a few hours sleep. We ride out at first light. It's time to end this." The longer this dragged on, the more he realized how badly he needed Lucy. Archie swore then and there: tonight was the last night he'd sleep without his wife by his side

.

Chapter Fifteen

When Lucy rolled over, Sofía was seated at the edge of her bed. There was something predatory in her eyes as she smoothed Lucy's messy curls. Lucy skittered away as quickly as she could, pulling the blanket up around herself. "What the fuck are you doing in here?" She demanded. Although Lucy's pregnancy wasn't obvious yet, she was worried about this baby in ways she could hardly fathom. Lucy shifted uncomfortably, "What do you want?"

199

"Pack your things. It's time for us to go." The expression on Sofía's face was completely devoid of emotion. "Time is of the essence."

Sickness roiled in Lucy's stomach and she inhaled sharply. "I'm not going anywhere with you," She snapped.

"Oh, yes you are. Otherwise I will kill your husband, your brother, and everyone you care about. Do not think I am bluffing. I would happily end the lives of these men and more to protect you, Lucy." Sofía's face remained permanently frozen in a smile but her tone dripped with icy venom. There was something dangerous in the way she remained ramrod still, almost as if she would lunge at any moment. "You have one hour to prepare. It is not safe here anymore..."

"What do you mean it's not safe?" Lucy needed to stall. There was a greenish hue to her skin as she tried not to inhale the cloying scent of Sofía's perfume. She silently pleaded with the baby inside her to settle down and cooperate. "I thought it was us against the world..." A sadness crossed Sofía's features so suddenly that Lucy would've missed it if she hadn't been staring straight at her. She'd obviously hit a nerve; the only thing to do now was press harder. "I don't know why you would want to leave this place behind after you worked so hard to build it."

"There are many things you do not understand, *querida*. I am your blood. I would do anything to protect you." Sofía's grey eyes misted with tears. "Your so-called friends robbed me and left. After everything I have done for them!" She shook her head angrily. "I can only imagine what horror they will unleash when they return for vengeance." It was the MC way. No sleight of hand would ever go unpunished. "They are my people, Lucy, I do not wish to kill them. I wished for them to be happy here…but if they choose not to be, that is on them. We will be many miles away by the time they arrive." Patting Lucy's shoulder once more, Sofía strode toward the door. "Pack your things. I will return for you soon."

A string of curses tumbled from Lucy's lips as the door slammed. Rushing to the bathroom, Lucy's knees ached from the force of falling onto them; she purged the remnants of last night's meager supper. After several minutes, she expelled nothing but bile. Lucy prayed for salvation as she tucked her legs beneath her and clung to the toilet bowl for dear life.

Cecelia must have reached Errol by now. Julia and Bea would be working with Steve. It was only a matter of time before the troops rolled in…but it was cold comfort. Sofía was clearly spooked and wanted to get the hell out of Dodge. It was even more important now that Lucy hold on as long as she could. It took quite a while before the nausea began to pass. Per Bea's instructions, Lucy took small sips of ginger ale, alternating with water to keep from dehydrating. Once she'd gathered enough strength, Lucy pushed herself up off the floor. She washed her face, brushed her teeth, and staggered back toward the bed for a much needed nap.

Sofía returned several hours later with a dark frown marring her features. "I told you to be ready to go. I do not have time to wait!" Walking to the edge of the bed, she intended to discipline her sister's child, but found herself staring into a pair of bloodshot eyes. She rested her hand on Lucy's forehead, brow creased with worry. "You have been ill."

Lucy swallowed hard and used the only weapon she had in her arsenal. "Sofía, I'm pregnant." She watched Sofía go from homicidal to nearly giddy with excitement. Lucy exaggeratedly rubbed her flat belly for emphasis. "I feel awful lately. I haven't been sleeping, I can hardly eat…I need time to rest, Sofía. I can't be out on the road in my condition." Lucy felt even sicker acting like she was some weakling who needed to be coddled; she was tough, despite the absolutely horrible way she was feeling right now. Still, Lucy couldn't argue with the results. Sofía was eating it up.

"My poor darling," Sofía cooed. For a long moment she said nothing as she mulled over her next move. "If you cannot travel then we must stay and fight. I will rally the troops." Sofía straightened her spine, as if gathering strength from her own decree. "This child is our blood and deserves to grow up in a safe place."

Lucy forced a smile. If being in the MC didn't work out, she obviously could make a living as an actress. "What better place than here, *Tía*?"

Sofía practically melted. "Of course, *querida*. You sit down and relax. I will have ginger ale and crackers brought to you—"

"I've got them. Don't worry." Lucy cut her off. The only thing Lucy really needed now was time to gather her strength. Sooner or later, her family was going to come for her and she had to be ready to go when they did.

"I will make all the arrangements. Do not worry about a thing."

As soon as the door was closed, Lucy locked it tight. She plopped down on the bed, drawing in deep breaths and trying to stop the stars dancing around her head. The bible sat on the opposite side of the nightstand and Lucy realized it was open. It seemed Sofía had helped herself to the book. She noticed a slight marking on the page, different from the code they used to communicate. An entire section had been highlighted…

"When you pass through the waters, I will be with you; and when you pass through the rivers, they will not sweep over you. When you walk through the fire, you will not be burned; the flames will not set you ablaze…" The passage read.

Lucy shuddered. An ominous feeling tugged at the pit of her stomach and it brought a new wave of nausea with it. Lucy wasn't a praying woman on principle…but right now, she could use all the help she could get. She begged whichever deity would listen that her friends had reached their destination and she would get out of here soon. Most of all, she prayed that Gabriel would come for her soon. This baby needed its father and so did she.

* * *

"Let's roll!" Archie's voice boomed over the sea of bikers revving their engines. The entire group had spent the last few hours gathering supplies and breaking into their assigned teams. Meanwhile, the leaders hammered out the final details. Archie and the Devils would ride in first, followed by Nightriders, the Redhawks, and Los Santos would bring up the rear. First up on the agenda was meeting with the FBI handler. Then, they would ride up to the Black Jacks compound and take down anyone who tried to stop them. It wasn't going to be easy, but time was running out.

Archie drew his pistol and fired a single shot into the air, signaling it was time to go. The thunderous hum of motorcycles that echoed in reply shook the ground. Riders began to move in groups of ten, leaving space between each battalion. The prospects from each club drove vans with extra ammo and supplies in between each cohort. Designated leaders within the groups carried radios, radioing to each other as they headed for their destination.

Danny rode beside Archie, his hands gripping the handlebars of his bike far tighter than was necessary. On his other side, Cecelia Santos barreled along in silence; she had insisted on coming with them and not a single man among them had the balls to tell her no. Cece's brother, Rogelio, was stationed in the back with the rest of Los Santos. Narayan stayed in the middle of the group, leading his men with quiet dignity. Adela had already returned home to the care of her mother and the relief was palpable. Marco and Candy remained aloof with one another, keeping several riders between them the entire trip. MC members of all shapes, sizes, colors, and creeds rode together as one to take down Sofía Salma and the Black Jacks. It was a marvel to behold.

Archie's jaw ticked as they rode deeper into the Nevada desert. It was not so sweltering now that summer had ended, but there was still something oppressive lingering in the air. It hurt to take a breath. What was worse, the closer they got to the meeting point, the uneasier Archie became. Up ahead he could see the outline of trailers and a group of heavily armed men standing at the ready. Although Archie had no criminal record himself, he knew there were quite a few parolees and men with dark pasts among them. Cops tended to make people nervous and he could feel a shift in the atmosphere as they pulled down the service road to the meeting point.

Steve stood beside Julia and Bea, chatting tersely as the massive sea of riders rumbled toward them. The dust cloud they kicked enveloped them, forcing Steve to cover his mouth with a bandana. "You should take cover," He hollered over the noise, gazing over at the girls. Bea immediately got into the car. It didn't surprise him in the slightest when Julia refused to budge; she tried in vain to keep her mouth covered with her hand. Steve sighed and handed over his own handkerchief without fanfare.

Jules accepted the offering with the barest hint of a smile. There were so many men out there, so many different patches; she had never seen anything like it. It was oddly exciting. When the first group parked their bikes and dismounted, Steve stepped forward and Julia remained glued to his side. When he cast a sidelong glance at her, she met his gaze with a challenge of her own. He wasn't going *anywhere* without her; the sooner he realized that, the better. Instead of arguing, Steve just shrugged and the two of them walked in sync, never breaking stride.

Steve greeted Archie warmly but was met with nothing but stony silence. Steve didn't take Archie's stoicism personally; if it was *his* wife who was locked up, he didn't imagine he'd be in a talkative mood either. However, it didn't stop Steve from trying to lighten the mood. "You weren't kidding when you said you had the manpower…"

"I'm not taking any chances." Archie's voice was gruff, a combination of aggravation and exhaustion. "I'm prepared to fight with everything we have." Reaching into the saddlebag on his bike, he pulled out the treaty Anita had drawn up. "I held up my end of the bargain."

Skimming the fine print, Steve folded the paper and jammed it into his pocket. "I've held up mine as well." He grabbed the radio clipped to his belt and gave the command. There was a fleet of military grade SWAT vans filled to bursting with riot gear, grenades, and every semi-automatic rifle known to man. "These are on loan. When this is over, they all get returned or I come after all of you. And believe me, this is only a fraction of what we've got." The threat lingered between the two men for a moment before Steve continued. "I've got men in the trucks ready to go. We'll be at my office, a block away from Aces High. It's a long way from the compound but if Sofía manages to escape, she'll head straight to the casino. Highway patrol is on standby."

"You really think she can get past us?" Archie raised a questioning eyebrow.

Julia's soft snort of laughter broke through the tension. Suddenly both men were staring her down and shrank back. "You're off your rocker if you think this is going to be easy. Sofía's got a backup plan for everything. She's paranoid and delusional but smart...worst of all, she thinks that she's doing everyone a favor by keeping those people locked up.

In her mind, the world is too dangerous a place for her girls." She licked her lips. "With Lucy it seemed to run deeper. Sofía made more of an effort. She never got beaten for defiance. Sofía even let her leave the compound long enough to meet with Stevie…that's unheard of."

If Steve minded Julia calling him *Stevie*, it didn't show on his face. He nodded curtly, "We believe this is due to the familial connection between them. Sofía wants family and loyalty and will use force to get it, if necessary."

"I'm sure it makes it worse that Lucy is—"

The air was knocked out of Julia's lungs as Candy barreled forward and smothered her sister in a hug. "Jesus Christ, I'm glad you're okay!" Candy gushed, the rush of emotions she had been holding back suddenly burst.

Archie gnashed his teeth. "Lucy is *what*? What's wrong with her?"

Julia looked stricken for a moment when she realized what she'd almost revealed. It was not her secret to tell, it was Lucy's. Thankfully, Bea picked the perfect time to appear.

"Jules just meant Lucy's still in there." Bea felt oddly disconnected from the scene at hand. These were not her people. She was never a part of their clubs; she was just another woman imprisoned by the

Black Jacks. Once upon a time she was a nurse working a night shift job at the local emergency room; her biggest concern was trying to sleep during the day and whether or not she'd get called in on her day off. Now, Bea had become deeply entangled in the battle against the most notorious biker gangs around. Her hand curled around the gun at her hip. How life had changed… "By now, I am sure Sofía knows we are coming. The longer we wait, the more time she has to shore up her defenses or escape."

Steve nodded curtly. "She's right." He extended a hand to Archie. "They move on your command."

Archie clasped Steve's hand tightly and shook it. He wanted to say thank you but at the moment, all he could think about was Lucy. The longer they waited, the more opportunity Sofía would have to hurt Lucy or worse. He wasn't going to let that happen.

Turning on his heel, Archie strode back to his bike. Steve, Julia, and the rest of Steve's team rode ahead; it would take them longer to get to Reno and set up communications. Once Archie was sure Steve was clear, he revved his engine and they were off.

Flashes of memory continued to plague Archie as they drew closer to the Black Jacks compound. Lucy was all he could think about: the tiny girl who'd reached out and held his hand when he was sad, the orphan with haunted eyes, the fiery-tempered prospect, and the gorgeous woman he'd taken to wife. Every experience had shaped Lucy into the incredible person she was today. Archie had fought his feelings for too long...when he got Lucy back, he swore he'd never take her for granted again.

* * *

The thick concrete walls of the Black Jacks' compound appeared in the distance, looming before Archie and the MC. The fortress stood alone, removed from the local town. Even from this distance, Archie could see that there were guards out front and snipers on the roof. Before he had a chance to warn them, Cecelia was radioing the leaders behind them. "Stay frosty guys, they know we're here!"

There was no doubt Sofía had the advantage. The first shots started flying when the Devils were still a quarter mile out. Archie swore bitterly and changed directions. The riot gear might stop a bullet but the impact of the shot would cause a wreck. Losing just one of their riders could cause a chain reaction that would take out a much larger group very quickly. The snipers standing at the top of the roof were trying to pick off riders in the middle of the pack. Parking his Harley off to the side, Archie grabbed his handgun and took off on foot.

Danny was at Archie's side in a heartbeat and Cecelia was only a step behind. They were bonded in rescuing Lucy from the Black Jacks. Cece dragged a hand over the blue strands of her hair and grasped

210

Archie's arm tightly. "Send the SWAT vans ahead and let the Black Jacks run their ammo out. When they retreat to refuel, we overwhelm them. If we break the group up and each take a side, we can take them."

"That's actually a really good idea. How the fuck do you know all this shit?" Danny stared incredulously at Cecelia.

"Not the time, *pendejo*," Cece chastised but she flashed him half a smile. There was no malice in her body language. She wasn't angry with Danny, they just had shit to do. Everything else would have to wait. Cece faced Archie again. "I know what I'm doing, trust me."

Archie nodded swiftly. "Danny, get it done," He ordered. "Cece, you're with me. You know the way in."

"Wait, that wasn't part of the plan," Danny balked, crossing his arms over his chest. "You're putting her in danger!" And for some reason, that made his chest tighten painfully.

Cecelia glanced between the two men. This was about to turn into a measuring contest and they didn't have time for that. "Danny, I'll be fine." She rested a hand on his shoulder. "We'll be in and out in no time."

"Then I'm coming with you!" Danny snarled, the protectiveness surging within him. "Lucy is *my* sister. I should be there!" He took a step forward.

Archie barked a sharp "*no"* in response. "I need someone manning the front lines, Danny. You're my second in command! If something happens to me, I need you to make sure that our guys get out. I need you to make sure *Lucy* gets out. Can I trust you to do that?"

Danny's face was molded into a mask of anger. "Why even make a plan if you were going to go cowboy all along?" He grumbled. Still, he grabbed Archie's hand and pulled him in for a tight hug. "You better get out of this alive. I'm not losing my favorite brother in law...you hear me?"

"I'm your *only* brother in law." A smile slid over Archie's features and he pulled back, clicking the safety off his gun. Danny needed a moment with Cece and Archie turned away to give them some privacy. In the meantime, he searched for a weakness in the compound's walls. The vans were already moving forward and bullets ricocheting off the metal seemed to be coming mostly from the front lines and the snipers on the roof. In the Southeast corner, Archie noticed a door they could get through with minimal exposure. It wasn't guarded on the outside, but he had no idea what was waiting for them inside.

Right now, Archie had to focus on Lucy or he risked being swept away by his rage. Cecelia broke into a dead run, keeping her head low as she made it to the side entrance. Archie was hot at her heels. The door was locked tight but she grabbed a slim pick out of her pocket. "Give me three minutes." Before she had a chance to touch the lock, Archie tugged her away and kicked the door open. "Or we could do it that way…" She grinned and allowed him to precede her into the building.

"Stop!" A shaky voice echoed down the hall. Priscilla's hands were wrapped tightly around a gun, her entire body shook as she aimed straight for them. "Put your weapons on the ground and back away!"

Archie growled low in his throat. On the one hand, he needed to get to Lucy sooner rather than later but he did not want to take out the women Sofía had locked up here to do it. Archie knew how brainwashed some of the women in Sofía's cohort were; he'd seen them at Aces High, blindly following her every command. Before he had a chance to react, he felt Cecelia's hand against his shoulder, urging him onward. "Go," Cece commanded. "I've got this."

"I'll shoot!" Priscilla's high, breathy voice stabbed through the earsplitting haze of gunfire and shouting from outside.

Vaguely, Archie heard Cecelia laugh as he rounded the corner. There was no doubt in his mind Cece

213

could handle herself…he just hoped it wouldn't end in bloodshed. Keeping his gun at the ready, Archie weaved his way down the long hallways, searching frantically for any sign of his wife. "Lucy!" He hollered, gazing down the twisting corridors. It took several minutes before he happened upon a massive room filled with bunk beds. He could hear muffled voices, women and children crying, but he couldn't see anyone. They must have been hiding in the rooms down the hall. "Lucy!" Archie hollered again, his fear rising as he glanced around. The area looked deserted but he could hear a whisper of movement rippling within the room. He wasn't alone…

"I know you're here," He snarled through gritted teeth. Silence was his only response. Creeping closer to the edge of the room, he felt a rush of movement at his back. A cold, derisive chuckle emanated from behind him. He turned to find Sofía with a gun trained on him.

"Drop your weapon," Sofía commanded. Her face contorted into a violent grin that made her entire body seem twisted. When he didn't immediately comply, she took a step forward and pressed the barrel of the gun against his chest. "I'm looking for any excuse to shoot you, *mijo*. Don't tempt me."

"Why don't you then?" Archie stared her down. The grayness of her eyes mirrored the blackness of her soul. "You orchestrated all of this. The violence at our borders, getting Lucy and I to come here, and making her gamble her life away to save mine. It's always been about Lucy." He gritted his teeth. "You don't give a shit about me. It'd be easier if I were dead so come on, finish the job!"

"Brave boy," Sofía chuckled darkly. "You remind me so much of my Hector. Strong-willed, determined…and willing to risk the lives of your wife and child for the good of your club." Her expression darkened. "Lucy is safe here. She has friends and family."

Archie's hands were clenched in fists of rage. It took every ounce of strength in his body not to tighten his finger on the trigger of his gun. "*We* are her family, Sofía! I'm her husband, Danny is her brother, and the Devils—"

"Treat her like garbage!" Sofía interrupted, her anger spilling over like lava erupting from a volcano. "Do you think I do not know what she has suffered? I have watched you. I see the way you treat her like she is nothing. You push her out of club business as if she does not belong!"

Guilt speared through Archie's chest. "I just wanted to protect her, Sofía!"

"Then we want the same thing," Sofía countered. "The only difference is that I can accomplish it and you cannot." Silence hung between them for a moment as Sofía circled him like a hunter stalking its prey, "I have everything here she could ever need: a medical facility, housing, food, an art gallery, commissary…what more could anyone ask for?"

"The people she loves!" He roared.

"Daniel is welcome here at any time!" Sofía countered. "But you," She pointed an accusing finger at him, "I saw Erik Archer only once. It was the day he gloated over killing my precious daughters!" Spiraling into despair, she suddenly sagged. "You will do the same to her. You will ruin her and you will ruin your child!"

Archie's shock was twofold. He knew his father had spent time in this part of the country, but he'd eventually settled in the South. It made sense now as to why his father never came back…killing kids was not something the club ever condoned. Erik had likely been banished and forced to seek asylum with another charter. Then, there was the way Sofía talked about a child. When she first mentioned it, Archie thought she was speaking abstractly but now it seemed too personal… "What are you talking about?" A new terror spread through him at the realization. "Is Lucy…" Sofia's expression was all the confirmation he needed. That's what he had been missing…and it only strengthened Archie's need to protect his wife.

Amusement had replaced Sofía's rage. She was totally unhinged. "It is not too late. Walk out of here, take your people, and go…there will be no retaliation." She leaned against one of the bunk beds, her expression unreadable now. "Or you will die today. I will not stop until every last one of your men is dead." There was a beat of silence as she stared him down. "No one else has to get hurt...walk away and you're free. Or I will crush you. Make your choice."

"I am not leaving here without Lucy." Archie steeled his spine.

"Suit yourself." Sofía raised her gun again and cocked it.

A single shot rang out, the blast echoing through the cavernous room.

Time seemed to grind to a halt as the soft thump of a body hitting the floor reached Archie's ears. Drawing in a labored breath, his body flooded with emotion. Life flashed before his eyes before he teetered, staggering under the weight of crushing relief.

Lucy stood on the opposite side of the room with her weapon drawn, silvery smoke rising from the white-hot barrel of the .45. Sofía crumpled, wide-eyed and shocked. The bullet had gone clean through her shoulder and blood polled onto the carpet, the circle of blood expanding with each passing moment. Archie turned to stare at the drawn, pale version of Lucy standing before him and he rushed to her side.

"Luce—" Suddenly and without warning, she pitched forward. Archie managed to catch her. "Lucy!" He cried as she lay limply in his arms. Her onyx eyes fluttering shut as he lowered her gently to the ground. Glancing up at the barren room around him, he yelled at the top of his lungs. "Help! Someone help!"

Chapter Sixteen

Once it had been discovered that Sofía Salma had fallen, all the fighting stopped outside. Those from whom she collected debts and held ransoms were free—she could no longer hurt their loved ones. Although the wound to Sofía's shoulder was not life threatening, she was being taken to the hospital to be patched up before they brought her to court. Steve was on his way to read the charges against her and start the process of her indictment. Slowly, the frightened women that Sofía had forced to stay in this prison began to trickle out to reunite with lost loved ones or start their journeys home. It should have been a happy occasion...unfortunately, for the Devils, they couldn't relax until they knew Lucy would be okay.

Lucy was vaguely aware of a murmuring voice pushing through the depths of her subconscious mind. She tried to move toward it, the sensation reminded her of trudging through mud. As she clawed her way toward lucidity, Lucy realized it wasn't just one voice surrounding her...there were far too many to count. Onyx eyes squeezed tighter but the harder she fought, the more exhausted she became. It wasn't long before she felt herself slipping away again. It was no use; she was powerless.

Danny shoved people aside as he collapsed next to the stretcher on which Lucy was strapped. "Lucy!" He cried, grasping her face. Archie sat on the other side, just as pale as Lucy. Danny wasn't sure who was worse off at the moment. He grimaced at the small moan of pain that emanated from Lucy's throat when the paramedic put an IV into her arm. Seeing his baby sister in this state was worse than any pain he'd ever experienced. Storming over to Archie, Dannie grabbed him by his cut and shook him. "What the hell happened to her?"

"I don't know…one minute I was arguing with Sofía and the next, Lucy shot her and collapsed." Archie's grief was palpable as he stared down at his wife's frail form. Lucy hadn't been hit by a wayward bullet, which was his first concern. The second, gut-wrenching fear was for the baby she was carrying. He'd only just learned of her pregnancy and it was already in jeopardy. Archie was trying not to think the worst. The only way they were going to know what was wrong was to get Lucy to the hospital. Nothing else mattered now except getting his wife the care she needed.

Cecelia tugged Danny away from Archie. He was working himself up and it was only a matter of time before somebody snapped. "Hey, he had nothing to do with this. Back off," She commanded. Danny was teetering on the edge of losing control. When he didn't immediately respond, she grasped his face between her hands and forcibly held his gaze. "Listen to me, Lucy is strong. She's much tougher than you give her credit for. She's going to pull through this, Danny."

After their parents died, Lucy had been the anchor holding Danny in place. If anything were to happen to her, he'd never recover. He looked ready to blast Cece...but then, he pulled her into his arms. Danny buried his face in the crook of her neck and inhaled the soft almond scent of her shampoo. In turn, she slid her arms around him, comforting him as best she could.

Archie breathed a small sigh of relief that Cecelia seemed to be keeping Danny balanced for now...but if Lucy didn't come around soon, there was no telling how bad the fallout would be.

"We've got to move," The paramedic urged. They'd already made it very clear that only one person could ride with Lucy to the hospital, but there were many who were willing to go.

"I'm her husband," Archie waded through a sea of people, barking orders as he went. "Danny, I need you to send our boys home. Tell the prospects to get everything the FBI loaned us back into the vans. Steve will catalogue them..." He paused a moment, facing Cece. "Help him, please?"

"I ain't a Devil, *jefe,*" Cecelia fired back but her posture changed when she glanced back at Danny's haunted face. "But...you said please. So, I'll make sure it's done."

Archie nodded a silent thank you and jogged to where the ambulance was parked. Lucy was loaded into the back and strapped in for the ride. The minute the sirens began to wail, the sea of bikers parted to let them pass. Vaguely, he was aware of the two paramedics staring in awe of the mass in front of them. "Have you ever seen anything like it?" One whispered to the other. The answer was unequivocally 'no'. Every motorcycle club within a thousand miles fighting for a singular cause was still baffling to Archie and he was the one who arranged it all.

As they drove past, Archie noticed Rogelio cross himself in a silent prayer for Lucy, Narayan bow his head, and Tim clench his fist in a display of solidarity. Everyone was pulling for Lucy, no matter what colors they wore. Archie hoped he hadn't used up all his miracles already...he just needed one more.

Exhaling sharply, Archie rested his head against Lucy's hand. She was warm despite the pallor of her complexion; it gave him the smallest ray of hope. "Come on, Luce," He murmured softly. Closing his eyes, Archie begged God to save the woman he loved so very much. When he opened his eyes again,

221

they'd arrived at the hospital and several nurses were waiting to bring Lucy into the trauma room. He was forced to stay in a crowded waiting room filled with crying babies, sniffling wives, and sad, stoic men. It was hell on earth.

Minutes ticked into hours and Archie's anxiety rose steadily. He paced the floor, muttering curses under his breath. One of the hospital volunteers offered him coffee and he accepted, if only to keep his mind sharp, but the toxic sludge made him jittery. He nearly flipped his chair over when he heard his name called over the loudspeaker. Rushing to the check in desk, Archie's heart was beating wildly in his chest. "I'm Gabriel Archer! Is my wife okay?"

Bea smiled gently as she opened the door to admit Archie into the patient care area. Steve had to pull a thousand strings to make this happen but it was well worth it in her eyes. It felt so good to be back at work and caring for Lucy was vitally important to her. "Follow me, Lucy's right through here." There was no personal offense taken when Archie blew past her and jogged to the room Bea motioned to. He closed the door gently behind her, holding Lucy's file close to her chest. "Your wife is doing just fine."

"Then why isn't she waking up?" Archie stroked Lucy's cheek gently. Some of her color was starting to return now and a rosy bloom spread over her cheeks. All around him, machines were beeping and buzzing and whirring. He let out a shaky breath, "And if she's so *fine*, what are all these things for?"

"This one is monitoring Lucy's heart rate and oxygen level, this one is the IV pump, and that one—" Bea rested a hand on the monitor that was spitting out paper reports every few minutes, "Is for the baby. Lucy is wearing a band around her abdomen that's monitoring the child's heartbeat." Walking around to glance at one of the printouts, she grinned. "The baby is doing very well too, considering all the stress Lucy's been under. The OBGYN has already been in to perform the ultrasound for confirmation. I'm sure that Dr. Arbor will be happy to share the pictures, if you'd like to see…"

Archie felt his heart shatter as he inched closer, watching the rapid movement. "I…" His terror returned tenfold as he watched the baby's heart rate speeding on the monitor. "It seems really fast."

"It's normal, I promise." Bea rested a comforting hand on Archie's shoulder. "Lucy is suffering from dehydration and sleep deprivation. She was experiencing some morning sickness, coupled with stress and not feeling up to eating. The combination is taxing on Lucy's body." Leaning over the bed, Bea smoothed Lucy's dark hair. "After she shot Sofía, I believe Lucy finally felt like she was safe. The adrenaline that had been keeping her going started to wane and she shut down. It's going to take a little while to heal. With some rest, fluids, and a few good meals, she will be fine."

"Thank God." Archie breathed and collapsed in the chair at Lucy's bedside.

A smile tugged at Bea's lips. "They're going to keep her overnight. The OBGYN will check her out again tomorrow. If everything's okay, they'll plan to let her go tomorrow morning." Stepping back to give Archie some alone time with his wife, she paused. "There's a restaurant and gift shop on the second level. They'll have one of the volunteers deliver, if you want. I'm sure Lucy would like something more than applesauce and graham crackers when she wakes up. Not to mention, she'll kick my ass if she wakes up and you're not in tiptop shape."

Archie couldn't help but grin back at Bea. It didn't surprise him at all that she and Lucy had become friends. Bea's presence put him at ease, even though he still was on edge. "I'll keep that in mind." He rocked back on his heels. "Any news on Sofía?"

Bea shook her head. "She's still in surgery. The bullet went clean through her shoulder but the doctor was worried about shrapnel in the wound bed. They wanted to make sure they got all the pieces. When she's out, she'll be transferred to section of the hospital we normally reserve for inmates." She paused. "With all the testimony pouring in, Steve has got an airtight case. You'll never have to worry about Sofía Salma or the Black Jacks ever again. That's definitely one thing to celebrate." The phone in her pocket started buzzing, letting her know another patient needed something. With that, Bea slipped from the room and closed the door behind her.

Archie settled himself down in a chair by the bedside. The room wasn't awful but it certainly wasn't home. He glanced back at the woman in the bed and his entire body convulsed with shock to. Lucy's onyx eyes were open and staring right at him. "Lucy!"

Although her head was still fuzzy and arm ached where they had put the IV in, Lucy managed to push herself up in bed. "Hey…" Lucy's voice was raspy and hoarse.

Archie stood over her, his hand slipping into hers and gripping tight. "I thought I'd lost you…"

"Please. It's going to take more than that to get rid of me," Lucy chuckled weakly. When she noticed the look on Gabe's face, she instantly regretted the jibe. "Hey, come here." Lucy shifted to accommodate him. They'd been parted for so long now, she worried it might be awkward; yet the moment he slipped in beside her, it felt like proper order had been restored to the world. Emotion burned in her throat as she smoothed a strand of his sandy blonde hair. "Did everyone get out? Is Danny okay? Did everything work out with your truce?"

"Danny's managing, Cecelia is keeping him in line." There was a beat of silence and Archie genuinely smiled. "You should've seen it, Luce. We have a treaty with Los Santos, the Nightriders, and the Redhawks now. Everyone came out in force." Swallowing hard, he glanced at her, "But I don't want to talk about that. I need to know how you're feeling." He wondered how much Lucy remembered of the last few hours. "You shot Sofía, you know."

Lucy licked her lips. "I did…and I'd do it again in a heartbeat. She was going to kill you." Her hand fell to the still-flat plane of her belly, careful not to bump the censor. "I love you, Gabriel. I couldn't let anyone hurt you." Resting her head against the pillow, Lucy covered her face with her hands. "I didn't want to *kill* her. Death would be a release for someone like that. Sofía deserves to rot for her crimes." Her voice cracked painfully.

Archie smoothed the dark hair away from her cheek, "Look at me, Lucy." It took a moment for her to gather the courage and he could see the tears forming in the corners of her eyes. "What's wrong?"

"How much time have you got?" Lucy sniffled, aching to sink through the cracks in the hospital floor. "Everything that's happened: my patch, our marriage, going to Reno, being taken by Sofía…it's made me realize how stupid I've been." She her head again so he wouldn't see the tears splashing down her cheeks. "I almost threw away everything I have just to prove a point. I'm—"

"Pregnant?" Archie finished for her. "I know…" Reaching out, he gingerly covered her hand where it

226

lay on her belly. "Lucy, you've only been fighting for what you deserve. I, on the other hand, have been the world's biggest ass…"

Lucy grabbed a tissue from the bedside and dabbed her eyes, "Go on." Despite everything that had happened, she was eternally grateful Gabe was here. He hadn't bolted the second he found out about the baby either. It allayed at least one of her fears. Holding his hand tighter, Lucy met his probing gaze. "You've spent so much time pushing me away."

Archie sagged. "I know, Luce." He licked his lips. "I'm no good at this…I have a hard time opening up to people. You're practically the first girl I ever met and I've been in love with you for as long as I can remember." Stroking his thumb over the back of her hand, he felt as if his heart was on display in front of her. "I want you so badly, but then I remember my father and the terrible things he did to my mother and I." He swallowed. "I couldn't stand the thought of hurting you like that. I thought my love was a curse…" Archie shifted uncomfortably. "It took me almost losing you to realize *not* loving you was hurting us more than anything else ever could."

"I've been saying that all along, Gabe," Lucy murmured. She shifted to rest her head against his shoulder. "You are good and kind and loving. You're going to be an amazing husband and father. I wish it didn't take you so long to realize it."

"You've always been smarter than me, Lucy. It was bound to take me a little extra time to figure it out." Archie was inordinately careful not to get tangled up in Lucy's IV or the monitors. It took some maneuvering but he managed to cradle her against his body. Pressing a soft kiss to her shoulder, he smiled. "I just want to go home and start our life together."

Lucy snuggled tighter against Gabe. She nodded eagerly. Getting out of Reno was her first priority. Then again, she also wanted things in Errol to be calm. "What about the baby?" Her voice was so quiet it was a miracle he even heard her. "We should've been more careful—"

"Lucy," Archie cut her off swiftly. "I'm happy. Shocked, a little nauseous, and terrified, but *happy*." He smirked. "I guess we played it a little fast and loose on our honeymoon. Now that I think about it, I'd be suspicious if you *weren't* pregnant." He teased. "We're going to be a family and that's all the matters."

The soft laugh that bubbled from her chest broke the tension between them. "I want that too...but there's something else, Gabriel." She sighed heavily. "I *need* my patch. After all this, I have to be a Devil."

Archie tensed. "Lucy, if this entire experience has shown us anything, it's that this life in the MC is too dangerous. I can't do it. I need you both to be safe."

"What this should have shown you is that we have the power to do good in this world." Lucy wasn't going to back down. "Everyone around here thinks the Devils are criminals and thieves. Probably because that's what it used to mean to be a part of the MC. But it doesn't have to be that way anymore." She stroked Gabe's cheek gently. "We can do good in this world. Let's fight for those who need it most. Women like your mother, Gabriel, and children like you."

Archie felt as if he'd been stabbed in the gut. He sat up. Lucy's words were a blow he wasn't expecting but now that it was out there, he couldn't ignore the thoughts spinning in his head. What if there had been a man like him around when Archie was young? What would it have been like if his mother had a place to go where she knew she'd be safe from Erik? Life would have been very different for the both of them. "How would we do it?"

"If we revamped the bar, we could turn it into a safe haven. Instead of using the boarding rooms for sex and debauchery, we'd open them up to people who need them." Lucy smoothed Gabe's hair tenderly. "No more wild, crazy parties. No more weeklong benders. We make the Devil's Own into something we can all be proud of."

"It's going to take a lot to convince the club," Archie warned. They'd likely lose some of their members...it wouldn't be easy. But he trusted his wife above all else. "I'm on board. Whatever it takes,

Luce. I never want to worry about something like this happening again." Archie smiled as Lucy pressed a tender kiss to his lips. He could feel the joy flowing off her in waves. "When we get back home, I'll call a vote." There were other reasons he wanted the entire club assembled. "It's never been done but I am going to move we waive the wait period and make you all full members. Hunter, Mort, and Kyle were instrumental in all of this."

"That's a great idea," Lucy smiled but it was interrupted by a yawn. The exhaustion was still weighing on her but her stomach was protesting the lack of food. "I think I heard rumors about crackers and applesauce? Do you think you could get me some? I'm *starving*."

Carefully slipping from the bed, Archie shook his head. "I'll get you some real food. Bea said there was a restaurant somewhere around here. I'll take a walk over and pick up whatever you want. Anything you're craving?"

"I would probably sell my soul for a cheeseburger right now..." Lucy chuckled. "Anything with meat and cheese and extra pickles would do it, though." Pulling Gabe down for another kiss, she grinned. "Thank you." Once Gabe slipped from the room, Lucy eased her way into the bathroom, using the IV pole to steady herself. There were dark purplish stains marring the delicate skin beneath her eyes, she looked drawn and pale, and that was only her face. Lucy's dark hair was frizzy and flying in every direction. She groaned at the sight. Perching on the edge of the toilet seat, Lucy did the best she could to tame the beastly curls. She splashed a bit of water on her face, reveling in the coolness. She felt like a whole new woman.

When Lucy stepped out of the bathroom again, Danny was hunched over in a chair with his face in his hands and Cecelia was crouched beside him. Her heart leapt into her throat at the sight. "Danny?" Her brother launched himself into Lucy's arms. He hugged her so tightly that he nearly knocked the wind out of her. "Oof!" Lucy gasped.

"Hey, be careful!" Cecelia chastised and slapped Danny's shoulder to get him to give Lucy some space to breathe. "I tried to get him to wait but he was making such a damn fuss, Bea snuck us back." She glared at Danny disdainfully, though there wasn't any malice behind it. "We just wanted to check and make sure you were okay. Now that we have, I'm sure we should let you get some rest. Right, Danny?"

Lucy laughed softly, "It's okay, Cece." Danny was still holding on tight and she stroked the back of his head the way their mother used to do. "Hey, Danny?" She pressed softly.

"Hmm?" Danny asked, raising an eyebrow to glance at her.

"When was the last time you washed that shirt?" Lucy made no bones about grimacing at the smell of

231

it. "You smell worst than the dumpster behind Marge's on trash pickup day."

Danny visibly relaxed and chuckled throatily. "Well, at least I know you're going to live. If you have the strength to nag me about my laundry, you'll have the strength to hold on." Gently, he helped Lucy back to the bed and arranged the blankets around her, as if he were tucking in a small child. "By the way, where the *fuck* is Archie?"

Lucy caught Danny's hand and held it tightly. "I made him go get some food. He's been here the whole time, I promise." Her thumb slid over Danny's knuckles as she attempted to soothe him. "He's a good man, Danny. I love him and he loves me." A smile tugged at the corner of her lips as Danny sighed in exasperation. "We've known Gabe since we were kids. You know he's going to make an excellent husband and father."

"Yeah..." Danny murmured several curses under his breath before his eyes widened. "Wait, a *father*?" He stared her down.

"Yes, and you're going to be an uncle." Lucy smiled at Danny's incredulity.

"You're *pregnant*?" Danny's breath caught in his throat as Lucy nodded. There was half a second where his expression was blank; then his face darkened and he looked positively murderous. "I'm going to kill him!"

Lucy laughed despite the gravity of the situation. Danny's overprotectiveness knew no bounds. "Gabriel is my *husband*." Her expression softened. "It's been just you and me for so long, Danny. Won't it be nice to have family holidays and picnics and birthdays all together? You'll have a little niece or nephew to spoil. Trust me, this is a good thing."

Danny didn't look convinced but Lucy looked so joyful that he couldn't stay sour. "Well, if you're happy, then I'm happy…" He sighed, "But I *still* want to kill him." Gazing at her with a sloping grin, he added, "Could I maybe just rough him up a little bit?"

Lucy narrowed her eyes at her brother; clearly, that was a 'no'. Danny looked appropriately sheepish as she leaned in and kissed his cheek. She glanced over at Cecelia who was doing her best to stay out of the way. "I'm so happy to see you, Cece. I was so worried."

Cecelia felt a sense of relief wash over her when Lucy reached out. Stepping to her side of the bed, she hugged Lucy tenderly. "Hey, I'm just as tough as I look," Cece teased. Brushing a strand of her blue hair to cover the scar Sofía had inflicted on her, she stole a glance at Danny. "We may have busted out but *you* saved our asses, *hermana*. And you don't have to worry about shooting Sofía. Jules said they're giving you a freakin' commendation or something for aiding an FBI investigation." Cece chuckled. "Though I got to admit, I'm a little pissed I didn't get to shoot her myself."

Lucy smirked. "Sorry, I beat you to the punch." Hugging Cecelia again, Lucy realized that glances were being exchanged between Cecelia and Danny. Those looks told her there was something more roiling beneath the surface. Her smile widened. "Did you two come here together?"

"No," Cecelia replied tartly, as if the question was ridiculous.

"Yes," Danny interjected, talking over Cece.

Lucy smirked and raised an eyebrow at the two, who were now engaged in a silent battle of wills. "Well, I'm just glad you're here..." Cece and Danny. Well that was something Lucy never expected. Cece looked like she was about to deck someone when Lucy interjected, changing the subject. "Is everyone else is okay? Jules and Candy? Adela?" When Cece nodded, relief washed over her; it felt as if a heavy weight had been lifted from her shoulders. Life was just about complete with Gabe stepped through the door with a cheeseburger.

Lucy eagerly helped herself to the first good meal she'd had in weeks. Cece kept watch while Danny and Gabe talked quietly. It was obvious Danny was being bullheaded but Gabe wasn't backing down. Lucy knew Gabe and Danny would eventually come to an understanding...but tensions were still running high after they'd all been through. What they all needed now was a good night's sleep. "That was delicious," Lucy announced. "But now I need to get some rest, and so do all of you."

"I'm not leaving you," Archie argued. "Not when I just got you back."

"I'm not going anywhere either!" Danny huffed, his arms crossed defiantly over his chest.

Lucy let out an exasperated sigh. Both of the men in her life were acting like jerks. She glanced at Cece who was leaning against the wall. "A little help?"

"I'll take this one." Cecelia put herself between Lucy and Danny, her eyes narrowed dangerously at him. "You heard your sister." He opened his mouth to argue but she pressed a hand to his chest to quiet him. "Standing here watching her sleep is a waste of both your time. Bea will call if you're needed and you can be here in a minute flat." Cece shook her head. "There's a motel across the street. Come on, we'll get a room."

Danny wrestled against his instinct to never let Lucy out of his sight again. But the thought of getting a room with Cece was enough to pique his interest. As badly as he wanted to deny it, he was exhausted and it would be better for both of them if he let her rest. "I don't like this, but it looks like I have no choice." Walking around the other side of the bed, he pressed a kiss to the crown of Lucy's head. "When you're feeling better, we're going to have a talk about you two ganging up on me."

It would be a very short talk indeed. Danny had always needed Lucy's guiding hand to keep him on the straight and narrow. Maybe now that Cecelia was in his life, she wouldn't have to work as hard. Lucy could only hope. Hugging him once more around the waist, Lucy smiled. "I love you, Danny."

"Love you too, Lucy," Danny echoed. He turned and slung his arm around Cecelia as they slid from the room. Although Cece pushed his hand away the first time, when he reached for her again, she just rolled her eyes and let it happen.

As soon as Danny and Cecelia were gone, Archie settled in a chair beside the bed. "I'm never going to let you out of my sight again."

"That's going to make trips to the bathroom uncomfortable for both of us," Lucy teased. Slipping her hand into his, she smiled gently. "I just want to make sure you take care of yourself too. The Devils need their President at his very best and so do I. Promise me you'll get some sleep?"

Archie scrubbed a hand over his stubbled jaw. A good night's sleep, a hot shower, and a shave sounded fantastic. Once Lucy was home, he planned on sleeping for a week with her tucked at his side. For now, though, he'd settle for a nap in a hospital chair. "I will," Archie brushed his lips gently over hers. "I'll be here when you wake up. I love you."

Although the starchy hospital sheets and thin blanket were not the most comfortable, Lucy was far too tired to care. "I love you too," She murmured, moments before sleep claimed her again. Archie was not far behind, resting his weary head against his palm. Despite the hustle and bustle of the emergency department, they only managed to catch a couple hours of sleep. It was definitely time to go home.

* * *

The following morning, Lucy was discharged from the hospital on the promise that she would follow-up with her doctor once she got back to Errol. She said a tearful goodbye to Bea and Julia, both of whom elected to stay in the city. Bea was overjoyed to be back working in the emergency room and Julia felt it was her duty to help Steve solidify his case against Sofía—whether he wanted her assistance or not. Gabe made preparations for one of the prospects to take his bike back to Errol; it wouldn't do to have his pregnant wife on the back of his Harley for several hours. Lucy needed rest and that meant trusting a prospect with his most prized possession. Well, second most prized now that he had Lucy back.

While Gabe was preoccupied with giving Hunter instructions about his motorcycle, Lucy snuck to the

237

stairwell. Bea let it slip that Sofía was being housed in a wing reserved for violent criminals, located on the fifth floor. When Lucy reached the ward, she found it was practically deserted except for a singular nurse, an aide, four security guards, and a janitor. While the guards chatted quietly about football, Lucy slipped into Sofía's room and closed the door behind her.

Sofía's shoulder was bandaged tightly and she wore a sling to keep it immobilized. An IV hooked on the opposite side along with a pump gave Sofía pain medication on demand. Formidable as she usually was, Sofía looked small and weak, her skin pale with anemia. She lay limply in the bed, staring out the window into the hazy midmorning sunshine.

"You can come closer, *mija*." Sofía's voice was soft and raspy. She gently rattled the metal handcuff at her wrist. "It's not as if I can come after you like this." Coughing slightly at the dryness of her throat, Sofía licked her parched lips. "Could I have a sip of water?"

Despite Lucy's reticence to get any closer than she had to, she grabbed a pitcher of water from the bedside table and poured a glass. Offering it to Sofía with a straw, Lucy watched as Sofía drank thirstily. Once she finished, Lucy set the cup down. Folding her arms over her chest, Lucy cleared her throat. "I wanted to tell you, I forgive you."

There was only silence as Sofía's grey eyes locked with Lucy's onyx ones. "Why?"

"I honestly pity you, Sofía." Lucy's voice remained level as she walked around to the other side of the bed. "You wanted equality and respect…but the way you went about it was utterly wrong," Lucy inhaled sharply. "You can't keep people prisoner and expect them to love you because of it." She narrowed her eyes. "Why do you think Magdalena left? Why do you think she *never* talks to you? Why do you think my mother cut you out of her life? It was never about the club, Sofía. It was always about *you*!"

Sofía's eyes shimmered with tears. "I just wanted you to have a better life than I did…"

"And I *will*, Sofía. I have a husband who loves me. I have a brother who would follow me to the ends of the earth." Lucy's hand covered her belly gently. "Girl or boy, this baby will be loved for exactly what he or she is." A soft smile tugged at the corner of her lips. "So, I wish you no harm. I can only hope your time in prison gives you a chance to think about what you've done." With that, Lucy turned her back.

"Lucy!" Sofía let out a gasping breath as she tried in vain to sit forward. "I will get out eventually. And when I do—"

Turning on her heel, Lucy's posture was tight with anger. "*If* you do, you better stay away from me. I may forgive you for what you've done but don't think for a second I want you to be part of our lives. If I *never* see you again, it'll be too soon." She exhaled shakily. "Family isn't about blood, Sofía. Family is about those who choose to stand by you and build you up. It's about letting people live their lives, about not forcing your choices on them." Lucy narrowed her eyes. "Consider this goodbye. And if you *ever* come near my family again, the next bullet I put in you will *not* be in your shoulder!

Sofía chortled menacingly, "There is nothing thicker than blood, *querida*. Remember that!"

Lucy shrugged Sofía off. She really wanted to slam the door in Sofía's smug face…but that would defeat the purpose of sneaking in here. Instead, Lucy hurried to the stairwell, making it back downstairs before anyone was the wiser. Gabe was just turning the corner when she grabbed the bag of her belongings from the bedside. She'd made it in the nick of time.

"You ready to go?" Archie grinned. Lucy looked much better now that she'd gotten some rest and a good meal. There was a soft flush to her cheeks and he rested a hand at the small of her back. She seemed almost nervous. "Are you sure you're alright?"

"Never better," Lucy stood on tiptoe and kissed Gabe sweetly. "I'm just eager to get home." Gabe took the bag from her hand and carefully helped her into the wheelchair Bea had arranged to take her out of the hospital. Together, Lucy and Gabe headed out into the sunshine. It was a beautifully crisp autumn morning, a soft breeze tickled over her skin. Gabe's hands wrapped around her waist as he helped her into the van, eager to get them out of the hustle and bustle of city traffic and onto the open road.

Once Lucy was buckled in, Archie weaved his way through the city. He kept his eyes straight ahead as they passed by the hotel they'd celebrated their honeymoon in, the Aces High casino—which had been formally shut down, and the little cafe they'd come to love. Archie almost expected to feel a pang of sadness at leaving it all behind but he didn't. He was grateful they were going back to their lives in Errol. He glanced over at Lucy; she seemed preoccupied. "You're awfully quiet."

Lucy smiled gently as she focused her attention on Gabe. Her mind kept swirling with everything that had happened over the last few weeks. It felt like she was finally waking up from a terrible dream. "I'm just thinking things are going to be very different from now on."

"That's not necessarily a bad thing," Archie replied. Lucy didn't elaborate and he shifted uncomfortably in his seat. "Is this about *us*? Are you second guessing your choice?"

"Loving you isn't a choice, Gabriel." Lucy's hand slid over Gabe's arm. "It's something I feel with ever fiber of my being. I'm just worried about what's going to happen when we get back to Errol." She sighed. "You know I need a unanimous vote to get my patch." Lucy rested her head against her open palm. "Hunter, Mort, and Kyle are most certainly going to get patched. They were on the front lines the whole time. Everyone saw how hard they worked. Me? I was locked up in the Black Jack compound. How can they see me as anything but some damsel in distress?"

"Lucy, you *shot* Sofía Salma." Archie remained focused on the road but he stole glances at her whenever he could. "You organized the breakout of the most influential members of every MC around. You were indirectly responsible for a treaty between the Redhawks, Los Santos, the Nightriders, and multiple Devil's Own charters. That's basically world peace!" Archie chuckled, "If that wasn't enough, you somehow convinced the FBI to work with us to bring the Black Jacks down. We put the militant group of lunatics that killed your parents, who have terrorized this club, and endangered our town for decades down for good!" He chortled, "Yeah, I have no idea why they'd patch you!"

Lucy beamed. "Well when you put it that way, I guess I have a shot!"

Archie nodded. "I knew you'd be eager for a decision so I had Hunter call the club. They'll be ready to vote when we get back." Lucy glowed with joy and Archie felt as if his heart would burst with joy. All he ever wanted was for Lucy to be happy…and she truly was. "We've got at least another hour and a half before we're home, why don't you take a little nap? You want to be fresh for the vote…" And he wanted to make sure they followed all the doctor's orders.

On another day, Lucy would have called Gabe out on his overprotectiveness but he was right, she was tired The sun steamed through the windows, warming her skin as she snuggled into her seat and let sleep overtake her. The next thing she knew, Gabe was gently nudging her. Wiping the grittiness from her eyes, Lucy drank in the familiarity of Errol surrounding her. Before all this happened, she'd seen this tiny town as a curse that held her in place. Now, she was overjoyed to finally be home.

After a quick pit stop to shower and change, Lucy and Gabe headed off to meet their fate. The clubhouse buzzed with excitement as Lucy slid out of the van and stood at Gabriel's side. Kyle, Hunter, and Mort were pouring champagne. Danny was sitting in the corner, nursing a scotch; he rushed to greet them as soon as he laid eyes on his sister. Hugging her tightly, Danny ushered her into the War Room and prodded Beaver out of his seat.

Archie moved toward the head of the table and without a moment's hesitation, the rest of the club followed. As soon as he sat, the meeting began. "In the last few weeks, we've accomplished more than in the entire legacy of this charter." He rested his hand on the table. "We got rid of the Black Jacks. We made peace with our brothers—" He paused and smiled gently at Lucy, "And *sisters* in arms. But most importantly, we've learned to work together. That's why I think it's time we make some changes around here." A soft murmur moved through the crowd. "First of all, there has already been a motion made to vote on prospects at today's meeting. Given the circumstances, I think it's important we waive the requirements that state a prospect must have been among our ranks for a year. I propose we have a vote right here and now." His cobalt eyes swept over the group, "Any objections?"

There was only the sound of shuffling feet and hushed voices. Archie nodded curtly, "So it's settled then. We will vote on Hunter Evans, Kyle Ferris, Mortimer Lally, and Lucy Archer." The whispers grew louder and he cleared his throat. "We'll start with Hunter. All those in favor?" Unsurprisingly, everyone in the room raised their hand. Clapping ensued as Hunter was handed a brand new patch for his cut, denoting his membership as one of the Devil's Own.

Kyle was next, followed by Mortimer—there was never any question about their loyalty. The room grew silent as Lucy was left standing alone beside Gabe. "Before you all vote, I'd like to say a few words…" It wasn't traditional for speeches to be made; then again, Lucy was far from the typical prospect. "I know that some of you might feel pressured to vote my patch through because I'm the President's wife. Or because Danny is my brother…or even because my father was an important part of this club back in the day." Lucy took a fortifying breath. "I don't want you to do that." The confusion in the room only made her smile wider. "I want you to vote for me because I'm an asset to this club and because I deserve to wear this patch. I know that some of you think women are weak or that we aren't smart enough to be a part of this club. Some of you think I'm only good for *one* thing..." There was more random shuffling amongst the group. Lucy narrowed her eyes. "That's not the case. I'm not going to stand up here and preach to you about what you already know. You have to decide what's right." Lucy took a step back, "So, go ahead, then. Vote."

Archie wrapped an arm around Lucy's waist, pulling her close to him as he glanced around the room. "All those in favor of patching Lucy Archer as one of the Devil's Own...raise your hands." Silence hung over the room for a long moment and no one moved. Archie raised his hand and Monster was half a second behind...he'd learned not to vote against Archie the hard way.

One by one, each member of the Devil's Own put up their palm until only Danny remained. He muttered under his breath, wringing his hands. Finally, he let out an exasperated sigh, "You know what? Fuck it! *Fine*...you can have your patch!" Danny threw his hand in the air.

"It's settled then." Archie banged the gavel. "Congratulations to our four new members!" The group broke into cheers and applause, clapping the newbies on the back…except for Lucy, who got several firm handshakes and polite conversation instead. Archie cleared his throat. "Now that we've settled that, there's one more piece of business to discuss here today." His hand slid into Lucy's. "Sofía Salma and the Black Jacks tortured and killed and held hostages…but the reason they did it is almost worse than their actions. Sofía Salma pledged to help those in need, women on the run, and children who cannot fight for themselves." He licked his lips. "For a long time, this club has been about little more than drinking excessively, getting laid, and maybe doing a little work on your bike on the side." Danny guffawed loudly but smoothly covered it with a cough. Archie smirked at him. "I think it's time the Devils have a new legacy."

Lucy snuggled closer to Archie as she addressed the group. "We would redo the bar and make it into a place of refuge. We'd expand the dormitories, maybe add a second story—"

"Yeah, but how we gonna make money?" PJ interrupted.

"The write offs alone would pay for the renovations," Big Mike piped up. He already had his notebook out. "We could apply for government funding and there are tax shelters for nonprofit organizations. Give me a few days to work up the specs but I could make this work." He beamed.

Archie glanced around the room. "We can do something good. That doesn't mean we won't ride. It also doesn't mean we're not going to party our asses off after this meeting…it just means we're going to start doing better than our fathers did." He raised his hand one more time. "All those in favor?"

A resounding echoed through the room. Lucy laughed and wrapped herself tightly in Gabe's arms. He bent to her height, eagerly capturing her lips. All around them, the club members laughed, drank heavily, and carried on as if it were a normal day. But to Lucy, it was not a normal day at all. The Devil's Own, Gabriel, and her family were finally safe and happy. It was everything she'd ever hoped for and more.

Epilogue

Lucy swiped at the dark circles under her eyes as she stared at herself in the bathroom mirror. Never in a million years did she think she'd ever be so tired or fulfilled. A lazy smile slid over Lucy's face as Gabe wrapped his arms around her and pressed a gentle kiss to her cheek. "Morning," She murmured and snuggled closer to absorb some of his warmth.

"I wish it wasn't," Archie groused. His hands glossed over her curves, reveling in the soft sigh of pleasure that emanated from her throat. He began to kiss down the contour of her neck, his fingers grazing the sensitive orb of her breast…and the piercing cry of a

247

hungry infant met his ears. Although Archie was slightly disappointed at the missed opportunity, he chuckled. "Well, she has your timing," He teased. Stealing one last kiss, he rubbed Lucy's shoulders. "You finish getting ready, I've got her." He reluctantly slipped away, heading down the hall toward the nursery.

"I love you," Lucy called after him, gratefully.

Initially, Gabe was nervous about fatherhood. As Lucy's pregnancy advanced, he was terrified to sleep in the same bed and walked around as if the slightest touch could send her into labor or worse. It took a blowout fight and a trip to the doctor to put everything into perspective. Lucy had to say, once he became comfortable with her growing curves, the man had been insatiable up until the bitter end. After a harrowing twenty hour labor and some choice curse words, she delivered a beautiful eight pound, six ounce baby girl into the world: Amelia Louisa Archer. Gabe was smitten with his child from the moment he held her in his arms and that love had been unwavering ever since.

Lucy rifled through the closet, attempting to hurry through her morning routine. It was an important day for their family and the Devil's Own Motorcycle Club. As of last week, they had finished all of the renovations and had received licensure to open up Errol's very first safe haven for people in need. The entire structure of the clubhouse had been taken down to the studs and rebuilt with twenty new beds, a large kitchen area, and a playground outside. They also had installed a state of the art alarm system and a team of bikers providing round the clock security. There was no safer place around. This afternoon marked the grand reopening and everyone had been invited...it was time to celebrate all they had achieved. Lucy couldn't wait.

Rifling through her closet, she paused as she found the vibrant dress she'd bought in Reno. It seemed like a lifetime since the horror with the Black Jacks. With everything going on these days, she hardly thought about it anymore. The dress was perfect for this occasion, and after months of hard work she nearly had her pre-baby figure back. It fit like a glove.

A peal of laughter from the other room caused the smile on Lucy's face to widen. Gabe was always making Amelia giggle; they were two peas in a pod. Lucy hurriedly pinned her curly hair out of her face before she rushed to join her family in the kitchen. Amelia's chubby cheeks were rosy and pink as she kicked her dimpled legs. The baby hummed and sloppily accepted bites of rice cereal from Archie, slapping her palms against the highchair in a showy display of approval. Lucy chuckled as she tossed on her apron before bending down to give her daughter a kiss. "I'm just wondering if there is any cereal *in* the baby. It seems like you're wearing most of it, dear," Lucy teased.

Chuckling appreciatively, Archie took a moment to admire his wife. Lucy was smart, beautiful, and in spite of everything, she loved him. How the hell had he gotten so lucky? He never pictured himself as the doting husband and father. Hell, he never believed anyone would *want* him to be...until Lucy. She made him better. Ever since they settled into a life together, Archie knew true happiness. "You look gorgeous, Luce." He planned on showing her just how much he thought so tonight. Archie had decided not to mention he'd arranged for Anita to watch the baby after the party. Lucy needed a night off with her husband. They were *long* overdue...

"You're a charmer," Lucy smiled. "You go get ready. I can finish up here." Gingerly, she wiped the cereal from Amelia's chin and plucked her from the highchair. Amelia cooed happily and snuggled into mommy's shoulder. Lucy sang softly while she bathed Amelia and changed her into the soft pink dress she'd been saving for this occasion. By the time Lucy finished packing up the diaper bag, Amelia dozing in the car seat.

Archie met them out front, smiling at the image of his two girls dressed in their Sunday best. It was a short ride to the clubhouse and there were already several bikes in the parking lot. Mort turned out to be quite the chef and happily offered to cater the event to drum up business for his new restaurant; he was currently manning the kitchens and bossing around their new crop of prospects. Kyle and Hunter finished putting the last of the balloons outside to mark the entrance while PJ hung the sign out front. By the late afternoon, most of the club was gathered, laughing, and ribbing each other while they worked.

Lucy never expected the Devils to respond as well as they did to all the changes. Instead of drinking and debauchery, there were charity rides and community outreach programs. Big Mike had his hands full with managing the financials of everything, so much so that he'd taken Luis and Nathaniel on as apprentices. Grayson decided to go to college and get an advanced degree in social work so he could help with counseling. Even Beaver was starting to show his softer side; he couldn't stop grinning as he gave tours of the place to anyone who asked (and some folks who didn't). This endeavor had brought out the best in everyone, so far.

Lucy caught sight of Danny moping around by the food table. Slipping over to him, she rested a hand on his shoulder. "Hey."

Danny groaned. She already had that look in her eyes…the one that told him she was reading him like an open book. "Hey, Luce." He dropped kiss to the top of her head. Maybe if he could distract her, he could avoid the lecture. "This is a great party. Nico said most of the local businesses have already donated to the shelter. You just missed the mayor, she was *very* impressed."

"That's great news. So, why do you look like somebody kicked your dog?" Lucy's expression softened. "I invited her, Danny, but you know how busy she is." Danny tugged away from her and Lucy sighed. Danny hadn't quite been himself ever since he'd started spending time with Cecelia. She came down when Amelia was born and had spent a few days here or there with her "Devil Family"— as she called it. Every time Cece went back home, Danny ended up in a funk that lasted until she inevitably showed up again. "Why don't you just tell her you're in love with her?"

"I *can't* be in love with her." Danny shrugged Lucy off and stuffed another mini quiche into his mouth. "I've never even had sex with her. How the hell can you be in love with someone if you're not screwing them sideways?" He grunted. "You know what? Don't answer that." Danny hurried away before Lucy could dig any deeper. Cecelia was a very difficult woman to understand. Usually *he* was the one saying it didn't mean anything. Cecelia was different. He cared for her and it hurt when she rejected him.

Lucy watched Danny retreat into the crowd. All she'd ever wanted was for her brother to find someone wonderful. Lucy loved Cecelia like a sister. Unfortunately, Danny had fallen for one of the most stubborn women on the face of the earth. Lucy just hoped their story would have as happy an ending as hers and Gabe's did. In the meantime, there were more appetizers to be put out and she had several more donors to greet. Fixing Danny's love life would have to wait another day.

Archie remained focused on trying to fix a banner that kept falling. He handed Amelia over to Anita shortly after they walked in. Not that she minded. Anita was ecstatic as she scooped the baby up and cooed over her pink party attire. Archie signaled for Danny to help him get the banner rehung. Danny headed over, mumbling about women and Archie patted his shoulder. "I know what you mean…" Once they got everything back into place. Archie caught sight of Lucy flitting around the room like a queen and his heart swelled with pride. Thanks to Lucy, the Devil's Own would have a legacy to be proud of and, somehow, it made him love her even more.

As the afternoon wore on, more friends and familiar faces began to trickle into the party. Steve arrived with Julia and Bea in tow. Bea—having come off the night shift only a few hours ago, slipped toward the bedrooms to see if she could catch a nap before she went to mingle. Steve went to grab himself a soda. There was a long moment of awkwardness when Anita and Steve came face to face for the first time in eight years. "Anita! Oh…hi…"

A blush bloomed over Anita's cheeks as she cuddled baby Amelia closer. It didn't seem fair to use the baby as a buffer, but Anita didn't know what else to do. "Hey, Steve." Anita swallowed hard. "It's been a long time…you look good."

Steve's heart leapt into his throat as he took a step closer. Suddenly all formalities went flying out the window. Everything he'd been holding back came flooding to the surface. "There's so much I've been wanting to say to you since that night in DC. I can explain everything, I—"

"Anita, who's this?" Mort wiped his hands on his apron as he interrupted Steve's nervous chattering. He was very much looking forward to taking a break and seeking out Anita for some alone time. What he found instead was Anita looking tense. "I don't think we've met. I'm Mortimer Lally...Anita's boyfriend."

Anita's head nearly spun as she stared between Steve and Mort. Her cheeks were flushed red with embarrassment. Her ex-husband and boyfriend in the same room; it was about to get awkward in here. "Mort, this is Steve Ellis. He's my ex-husband." There was a long, deadly silence as she waited for Mort to react. Something akin to jealousy spread across Mort's features but, thankfully, he kept his cool.

"It's nice to meet you." Mort's arm wrapped around Anita's waist protectively. He extended his free hand and shook Steve's forcefully. "Thanks for all the work you did helping bring Lucy and the girls home." He forced a grin. "We owe you one, for sure."

Steve returned the smile hesitantly. "I was just doing my job." There was a short pause and he reached out, tugging Julia to his side. "This is Julia Amos...she's, uh, my girlfriend too. I mean, not *too*...she's just my girlfriend."

Julia's eyebrows shot up in surprise. "Uh, yes, girlfriend...*right*..." Well that was news to her. Steve was kind but he'd never given Jules the time of day. There was always some excuse as to why they couldn't be more than friends. The moment Jules laid eyes on the blonde goddess before her, she realized *exactly* what was going on. "You must be Anita, right?" Jules suddenly felt inadequate. Anita was beautiful and voluptuous and successful. Julia was...not. She was a natural redhead with a tendency to freckle and who blushed at every turn; not to mention her figure had always decidedly boyish. Now that she'd seen Anita, Jules was positive there was no way she could ever compete.

"It's so good to meet you, Julia." A sharp cry from the baby brought her attention back to the bundle in her arms. Anita was grateful for the distraction. "Looks like someone needs a diaper change. It was so nice seeing you two." Anita hurried to the room she'd stashed Amelia's diaper bag in. Although Anita didn't want to admit it, seeing Steve dredged up feelings she had been pushing aside for a while now. Eight years of buried feelings came welling back to the surface. It was going to be a long night...

Once Mort went back into the kitchen, Julia turned her dark glare toward Steve. "Girlfriend, huh?" Steve had the good sense to look sheepish but it wasn't enough for Jules. "We'll talk about this later. I just saw Candy sneak in, I'm going to say hello." Brushing Steve off coolly, Jules sauntered over to the corner that Candy was hiding in. "Hey sis," She leaned in

255

and kissed Candy on the cheek. Beside Candy stood her son, who clearly did not want to be at this event. Julia nudged him playfully. "Hey Matty. What's up, bud?"

At fifteen years old, the last thing Matthew wanted to be doing was hang out with his mother. But after being stuck in the Black Jack compound for months and then coming home to find the mess he'd gotten into in her absence, his mom wasn't letting him out of her sight. Matt rolled his eyes and tugged his phone out of his jacket pocket.

Candy hugged Julia tightly, ignoring her son's moody behavior. "This is a great turnout. Lucy's done such a fantastic job of—"

"Candy?" Marco's voice seemed to carry over the entire room as he paused in from of her. He'd been silently praying she'd show up tonight. Honestly, it was the only reason he came. His heart leapt into his throat when laid eyes on the young man she was with. There had been rumors that Candy had a son but he'd never been able to bring himself to look into it. Now was as good a time as any. "Who's this?"

"Hey kiddo, let's go check out the food table!" Jules announced and dragged Matthew away to grab a plate. She was strong but Matty was stronger, he put himself in front of Candy, his arms crossed over his chest. "Who are *you*?"

Candy's panic clawed at her. Fifteen years ago their relationship ended and she'd never found the courage to tell him she was pregnant. "Marco, this is my son Matthew," Her throat was suddenly bone dry. "Matthew, this is an old friend of mine, Marco." Shooting a desperate look at her sister, Candy silent begged Julia to get Matthew out of here. It took some maneuvering, but eventually she was able to drag the teenager away with promises of free food and sugary drinks.

Marco was silent for a long moment as he watched Matthew walk away. When he finally found the courage to speak, there was a note of fear in his voice. "Candy—"

"Marco…*don't*." Candy wished that things could be different but the past was the past. The lie she'd been telling for fifteen years rolled off her tongue with ease. "My husband and I were lucky enough to have a child before he went off to Afghanistan…" Candy was trembling.

"Really?" Marco frowned markedly.

Matthew had grabbed a couple things to eat but he couldn't help but sense how his mother's concern. Ignoring his Aunt Julia's pleas to stay away, Matty stalked over to where Marco and Candy were talking. "Look, dude, I don't know who you are but you're upsetting my mom. I think you should take a lap." He wrapped his arm tightly around Candy's shoulders.

257

"I'm sorry. Matthew, it was good to meet you." Something didn't feel right about this situation. The boy had his eyes... those sparkling, haunting, Caraway green eyes. Matthew had to be around fifteen years old, which meant Candy would've conceived around the time they were together. Even if the soldier she married had been with her in that timeframe, there was also an equal chance that kid could be his. Marco was going to get to the bottom of this one way or another.

"Hey, Matty, how about you get us some punch?" Julia pasted a smile on her face until her nephew's back was turned. Then, she rounded on Candy with murder in her eyes. "What the hell are you doing?"

"Protecting my family," Candy hissed. "I won't go down this road again!"

"It's been fifteen years." Julia whispered back, "Matthew never even *met* Anthony. After everything that's happened, Matthew *needs* a father in his life. Don't you think it's time you told the truth?"

Candy wrapped her arms tighter around her waist. "I need time to think about this. And if—and that is a very big *if*—I decide to tell them, I need to do it on *my* terms. I love you, Jules, but this isn't your secret to tell." Candy needed to get away...if only for a moment. "Excuse me." She headed into the bathroom for a moment of privacy.

The door to the clubhouse swung open again and, much to the surprise of everyone assembled, Narayan Bosko brought his wife and daughter Adela to the fundraiser. He drank punch, chatted about politics, and donated generously; he even offered the support of the Nightriders if their services were ever required. Tim Gunter was unable to make it personally but he sent along his nephew and several other club members to show his support. It seemed very odd that Los Santos—who had remained the closest after the takedown of the Black Jacks—were not present. At least not at first.

It was well into the evening when Cecelia and Rogelio Santos slipped in through the back. Rogelio looked a little worse for the wear, arm in a cast and several lacerations on his face. Cece quietly informed everyone that her brother been in a motorcycle accident earlier in the week and wasn't feeling his best. For once, she doted on her brother and made sure he got a seat near the food table; she'd even found a couple of Devil Eaters to keep Rog happy while she said her hellos.

Danny didn't even bother to play it cool when he realized Cece had arrived. He rushed over, grabbing her in a tight hug. Cecelia laughed and let it happen for half a minute before she shrugged him off. "I'm here now, *pendejo*, now the real party can begin!" Cece nudged Danny playfully before they went to grab a couple drinks.
The sight of Danny and Cece cozied up in the corner made Lucy smile. It seemed that everything was

working out after all. Lucy slid beside Gabe again; he draped his arm around her and she beamed. "I never thought I could be this happy…" Lucy murmured. "That's all thanks to you."

"No, it's thanks to you. This is all your doing." Archie grinned. "I will never be able to make it up to you in a thousand lifetimes but I'm going to try. Lucy, you were right all along. You are exactly what this club needed…and what *I* needed." Kissing her sweetly, he grasped her hand and began tugging her toward the door. "By the way, Anita is going to watch Amelia tonight." He whispered into her ear, "I've got a big evening planned. A moonlit ride along the river, a hot meal that we eat without being interrupted, and…then I think we should get started on baby number two."

Lucy captured Gabe's lips again. "There's nothing in the world that would make me happier." Hurrying out to the van, Lucy stopped to gaze at Gabriel standing in the soft glow of dusk. Somehow, despite the odds, all her dreams had come true. It might have taken a little gambling to get it done, but the results could not be argued with. "I love you, Gabriel."

Archie captured her lips once more, "I love you too, Lucy." And with that, they headed toward the vibrant red sunset. Happily ever after was right around the corner.

The End